JCJC, JSTO

HELEN GRIFFITHS

GRIP
A Dog Story

illustrated by Douglas Hall

HOLIDAY HOUSE · NEW YORK

Text © Helen Griffiths 1978
Illustrations © Hutchinson Junior Books 1978
First American publication 1978 by Holiday House, Inc.
Printed in the United States of America

Library of Congress Cataloging in Publication Data

Griffiths, Helen.
Grip, a dog story.

London ed. has title: The Kershaw dogs.
SUMMARY: A young boy experiences conflicting
loyalties for his father, a breeder of generations of
champion fighting dogs, and the playful pup he loves
so much.
[1. Dogs—Fiction.   2. Fathers and sons—Fiction]
I. Hall, Douglas, 1931-   II. Title.
PZ7.G8837Gs 1978   [Fic]   78-6819
ISBN 0-8234-0335-1

Contents

Madman

Madman was Bill Kershaw's dog and those that knew him said that he was well named. Anyone who saw him in the pit, even before a fight had started, observed him with a respect not untinged with fear. He weighed a good fifty pounds and all of it was muscle because although Bill Kershaw fed him well he also worked him hard, and to witness his ferocious excitement before the start of any fight was to realize that he lived only for the savouring of battle and battle itself. With lopped ears pressed against the big white head, and slanted small eyes that gleamed with a mad light at the sight of any other dog, there was that look of an alligator about him which struck fear into the heart of any civilized being.

He had never lost a single fight in the five years he had been seen in the pit and he was more than a champion fighting dog. He was almost a legend. Rumour had it that Bill Kershaw had turned down an offer of two hundred pounds for him – more than a man could earn in a year! But Bill Kershaw could no more sell his dog than he could his son, although some people wondered which of the two he preferred.

A sportsman from Birmingham made that offer (so it was said, because Bill Kershaw was a tight-lipped man who gave nothing away and was as surly as his dog was mad) and when it was turned down he persuaded Kershaw to take his dog to Birmingham where the prize money was greater than in his native town.

The West Midlands were a long way from Yorkshire but Madman's fame had travelled that far. He was talked about in all the dog-fighting circles of the north and some even said that London knew about him, but this was only talk without foundation. Madman fought in Birmingham for a year and made enough money for his master to buy a small public house back in his home town. Dogs were brought to him from as far away as Leeds and Rochdale and from across the Lancashire border and Madman crippled or killed them all. He never left a whole dog in the pit.

Yet this was in the 1930s, more than twenty years after the Protection of Animals Act of 1911 expressly forbade the keeping of fighting animals or premises for their use. Bill Kershaw knew about this Act and ignored it, as did all those dog-fanciers who brought their animals of a Saturday or Sunday to challenge his Madman. It was all done in secret and, often as not, the pit was marked out in stones or sawdust on the moor at a place mutually agreed upon only hours before to keep the police from getting wind of it.

Bill Kershaw was justly proud of his dog whose pedigree he knew better than his own and which went right back to the bull-baiting days of the previous century. Madman, as much in conformation as in character, was the best in Bull-and-Terriers to be seen in either North or Midlands. Present-day fanciers were concentrating on their looks now that fighting was no longer permitted by law but they were still anxious for Madman to sire their stock. They knew he was a killer and wanted to keep the spirit there. Bill Kershaw made them pay for it.

On more than one occasion he had been offered the pick of the litter instead of a stud fee but he always took the money because Madman wouldn't tolerate another dog in the house. However, as time went by, even he had to admit to himself that there had to come a day when Madman would be finished. He couldn't go on for ever. Besides, his son was getting to an age when he could bring on a dog himself and he instinctively wished to continue the cycle which had begun long before. Everyone knew that the Kershaws kept fighting dogs and everyone knew, too, that they only kept winners.

'So this dog's got to be a winner, too,' he told the boy. 'Happen the best thing would be to bring on one of Madman's sons. Next time he's crossed with a good bitch I'll take the pick of the litter.'

So it was that early one Sunday morning late in March Bill Kershaw and his son Dudley set off on the five-mile walk to a cotton town just over the border where a bull-terrier bitch had recently whelped a litter of Madman's offspring. It was a long, cold walk across the moor in spite of the sun, with the wind blowing against them all the way and, in many places, snow crunching under their boots. Both of them were thinking with keen interest on the pups they were going to see and neither of them spoke above a word or two.

Dudley was the image of his father, his dark, almost black hair as stiff as a pony's, its short cut under his cloth cap giving a brutish expression to his face which, with its heavy eyebrows, made him look as churlish as the man beside whom he strode, eyes half closed against the wind, shoulders hunched. He was eleven years old that winter but acted little like the average boy of his age and was very much a loner, partly because his home was isolated but mostly because his father had never encouraged him to make friends.

Bill Kershaw himself took a harsh pride in his aloofness from the people round about. His wife had run away from

him years earlier, when the boy was only a toddler, and
this shame had caused him to cut himself off from those
who would sympathize with him as well as those who
might secretly be laughing at him. He brought the boy up
on his own, with help from no one, and only reluctantly
sent him to school, because the law demanded it. The one
true passion of his life was fighting dogs and this also kept
him apart from his neighbours. It was a secret passion,
only to be shared with those who understood it, men who

had dogs of their own to pit against his in spite of the law. He had no time for small talk, not even behind the bar of his own public house where he rarely drank with the customers, and usually only opened his mouth when he had something that needed to be said. He wasn't even eloquent about dogs.

Dudley could not help but develop in the same way, from a lonely, half-neglected infant to a silent, self-contained lad. He had no friends at school because he had no sense of humour. His answer to every affront, whether real or imagined, was to use his fists. Therefore the boys were wary of him and kept out of his way and the girls were frightened of him because of his reputation. For Dudley, like Madman, had his reputation, earned by his looks and his actions.

'You want to keep away from that Kershaw boy,' most mothers told their children. 'Both he and his father are a bad lot.'

'A bad lot' summed up what most of them instinctively felt without being able to say exactly what was bad about them. They were both so silent and pugnacious, with glowering brows and hard expressions, that they successfully kept the world about them at bay.

They lived a couple of miles outside the town at a place called beautiful because it was like an oasis between the barren moor and the soot-black mills and houses. In the summer months people would spend the day there, paddling in the river which flowed strongly over its stony bed, picnicking in the woods which were waist high with ferns. The wood gradually sloped upwards and petered out as slate rocks took over, towering above the trees with the moor beyond. Water oozed down these crags both summer and winter and the rocks were green with mosses and slime. In good months a few cattle usually grazed at the foot of the crags, among the grass and rushes, but the earth was boggy and soft and not too good for their hooves.

Bill Kershaw kept the only public house along that road, called The Crags, and when the picnickers came he did good business, with a tea garden at the side for mothers and children where Dudley served them bottles of pop and ginger-beer as well as tea and milk. But for much of the year business was bad. No one went to The Crags when the sun wasn't shining or it wasn't a holiday, no one except the men who shared his passion for fighting dogs. They had a few drinks and talked about fights, and now and again they organized sports of other kinds on which they could bet their money, hard-earned in the woollen mills or miserably dished out at the dole office, sports for which Bill Kershaw's isolated inn was the ideal place.

In the cellar, among the barrels of beer and crates of soft drinks, they set their dogs on rats and badgers and the money changed hands as the blood flew amid growls and squeals and shouts of excitement. They were all men hardened by lives of oppressive poverty, disillusioned by war and unkept promises, and in this way they could forget the wives who nagged them and the problems that beset them. Sometimes they lost a few shillings, sometimes they gained them. Sometimes they would lose a dog but they soon found another from somewhere, though not all of them were good enough to match in the pit, the only place where a dog's gameness could really be tested.

By the time he was eleven Dudley understood almost as much about a good dog's qualities as did his father. He had seen animals which looked brave enough, snarling and lungeing at others while on the leash yet refusing to come up to a second round with an unleashed adversary. He had seen those with a courage as big as themselves but without the stamina to match it, and others with plenty of both. It was only the latter that triumphed in the end, so he knew as well as his father that Sunday that he had to choose a pup with both guts and strength if it were to be any good.

Dudley had never seen a puppy before. Madman had come to his father when he was going on for six months old and he had taken him against a debt that hadn't been paid. His previous owner had neglected him and he was all jaws and ears, with ribs that stared through a patchy skin. Bill Kershaw fed him up on raw meat and eggs and when he was strong, with no ribs to be seen, he cropped his ears to save them from being torn off in fights and so as not to give an adversary something to get hold of. It wasn't until his first fights that his true nature began to show and the only time Dudley ever saw him in a state of excitement was when he knew there was going to be a fight and he could hardly contain his impatience to be shown his adversary. Even in those early days, which Dudley could hardly remember, there had been something about his eyes that chilled him, that made him feel afraid of his father's dog.

As he tramped across the frozen earth, hands pushed down into his pockets, ears almost senseless with cold, he wondered what Madman had looked like as a puppy. Did puppies have that malevolent expression? Did those he was going to see already fight among themselves?

He knew that the mother of the pups had proved her courage in the past. She had been used as a pit dog for more than a year before being retired for breeding, otherwise his father would never have considered bringing on one of her pups in Madman's footsteps, not even though he had the certainty of his sire's blood.

'People are getting soft these days,' Bill Kershaw told his son. 'They only want dogs for showing. Mind you, I've nowt against a good-looking dog but what's the use of looks if the character's missing?'

The scorn in his words had impressed itself on Dudley

and he knew he mustn't choose the puppy for its looks alone.

'Remember, he's going to be thy dog,' he had said. 'Thee'll be the one he's got to look to for food and orders. If tha chooses a wrong'un, it'll be thy responsibility. Tha'll never learn for thyself if I do the choosing and the work.'

'Suppose I don't know how to choose?' he had asked, half-fearfully, because he could tell by his father's words that he was expected to know.

'Then tha's not ready to have a dog,' was the curt reply, 'and I'll take the brass instead of a pup.'

That morning, before they set out, his father had asked him, 'What are we going to do, have the dog or the brass?' and, feeling less sure than he showed, Dudley had opted for the dog.

He had thought about it half the night, unable to sleep, gripped by a suffusion of feelings he had never experienced before. Madman was his father's dog and he had shared his father's pride in him, but, apart from this, he felt nothing for him except perhaps dislike because the dog completely ignored him, and even a tinge of jealousy. He had never had anything of his own and he had always been alone, distrusting other boys, misunderstanding their words and actions. If he was lonely, if there was no gentleness in him, he was unaware of it and yet suddenly, thinking about the dog that was going to be his, without even knowing it, not having yet seen it, feelings he couldn't put a name to filled his heart and mind so that he couldn't sleep or even lie still until utter weariness at last defeated him unawares.

This morning, striding silently beside his father, those feelings returned, making him lose confidence in his ability to make the right choice. He wanted a dog as bold and as fierce as Madman and already he felt things towards that unknown puppy, things he couldn't explain.

14

The best of the litter

Sheets were hung across the cobbled street, billowing in the wind but not catching much sunshine because of the shadows thrown by the houses opposite, where Dudley and his father came down the steep hill into the town.

'Joe Barnes lives at twenty-three,' said Bill Kershaw, dodging between them, and Dudley felt his heart beat faster as he counted off the numbers on the doors. All the houses were alike, with black, stone walls, slate roofs, one downstairs window and one up, their chimneys smoking into the sunshine.

The bitch and her puppies were in the back downstairs room of number twenty-three and Joe Barnes stood over her when they came in, hands in pockets, not even pretending to hide his pride. There were old newspapers all over the floor and near the big kitchen range in which a fire was steeped lay Bess, mother of Madman's offspring.

Dudley only had eyes for the pups which, at going on for eight weeks old, were adventuring all over the room, growling and scrapping, pawing at table legs, chewing the corner of a rug. He should have been listening to what was being said about them but he was lost in contemplation. Every one of them was beautiful and they all looked much alike with their pink noses turning dark in streaks, their stiff tails wagging as they tumbled about.

One of them came up and attacked his boots. He

looked down, grinning delightedly, and gave it a push with his toe which made the puppy topple over backwards, taken by surprise. With a growl he scrambled up and pounced again.

'Aye, he's a lad, that one,' said Joe. 'If tha's not careful, tha'll go home minus a boot.'

'Can I pick him up?' asked Dudley, longing to feel that chunky, battling body in his hands, and as the man nodded he knelt down and grabbed hold of him.

'Look at him, Dad!' he exclaimed with pleasure. 'He looks just like Madman.'

The pup was now trying to nibble his nose and Dudley felt its warm tongue on his frozen face.

'What about the rest?' his father reminded him. 'Happen tha ought to look at them too.'

Smartly, Dudley set the pup down. He was here on business, not to laugh at a puppy's antics, but there was something about that roomful of gambolling, joy-filled creatures that made it very difficult to put his mind to serious choice. Bess watched them all anxiously. Did she know which was the best of her litter? he wondered.

You don't choose a pup that has to earn its living as a fighting dog in five minutes, so Bill Kershaw and his son accepted a cup of tea and, while the kettle boiled over the fire and china was set out and the tea left to mash for a while in the pot, they sat at the table and watched the pups. Bill Kershaw said nothing, his dark eyes keenly taking in the size and shape and movement of every white body that tumbled about, advanced or retreated. Now and then Dudley shot him a covert glance, hoping to judge by his expression what his feelings might be about a particular animal, discovering nothing because his father's face rarely displayed his thoughts.

They all had big ears and rolls of fat on their legs. They all looked tough and adventurous. Which one of them would be his? Which should he choose and, most difficult of all, how could he know if he was right?

When they had finished their tea Joe Barnes picked up the first of the dog puppies and placed it on the table, offering it to Bill Kershaw for examination. Bill pointed to his son.

'It'll be his pup. Happen he'd better choose it.'

So Dudley grasped them one by one and ran his hands over their loose little bodies, keenly trying to discover that hidden something that would tell him which pup would be his. They all reacted in much the same way, trying to chew his fingers, wriggling out of his grasp, blundering into cups and milk jug which hadn't been cleared away. Now he couldn't even remember which one he had originally picked up, the one that had attacked his boot with such ferocity. Desperately he glanced at his father for help.

'Look at their jaws,' he suggested. 'And don't forget bone and back.'

So Dudley looked at their jaws, trying to decide which had a head most like Madman's, and then he looked for a straight back and good bone and feet, and when he'd finished looking he knew which one he wanted though he didn't know why he wanted it. It was the third one he had handled and it looked much like the two previous ones and the one that came after, with overlarge ears and eyes like buttons, and he only hoped that his father wouldn't ask for an explanation when he chose it. He hardly dared hope that it was the one he would have chosen himself but he couldn't ask. That would show lack of confidence in his own judgement.

'I'll have this'n,' he said, picking it up for the second time.

The two men closely examined his choice and Dudley's heart beat anxiously as he wondered what they were thinking.

'Aye,' said Joe Barnes. 'Tha could've done worse.'

'We'll know better when we see how he shapes,' was all Bill Kershaw would say.

There was nothing wrong with its conformation and it seemed lively and healthy enough. As for its character, only time would tell.

'Come on then, lad. We've a long walk home,' he said, pushing back his chair.

'Put him inside tha jacket,' Joe Barnes suggested to Dudley. 'It's right cold outside.'

Dudley undid his jacket buttons and his own warmth seemed to close round that of the puppy as he felt it struggling against his chest, suddenly frightened at being held so close.

'Now, now,' he said softly, trying to calm it. 'Thee'll be all right with me.'

He saw the creature's anxious dark eyes looking up into his and smiled. 'Thee'll be all right with me,' he said again, and the puppy licked his nose, still frowning.

On the way back home over the moor Dudley, who in all his eleven years had never actively felt anything towards anybody, except perhaps pugnacious dislike or suspicion of his schoolmates and a fearful respect for his father, fell in love with that puppy pressed against his chest, its damp nose tucked under his chin. As he jumped from tussock to tussock of grass over the moor, following streams when the footpaths disappeared for fear of stepping into hidden bogs, clinging to the puppy to keep it steady, he let his father get a long way ahead, not wanting his company.

He might just want to talk about the dog and Dudley didn't want to talk, too full of feelings to have anything to say. There would be time enough when they were at home and he had got used to the idea of having a puppy that was solely his, to examine and talk about him dispassionately. By then he would have mastered this confusion of heart and mind, which he somehow suspected to be wrong although he couldn't help it.

He didn't want his father to know, didn't want him to see the delight that was in him. Perhaps it was because he had so little faith in his own judgement or because he had never done anything so important before, but just then he couldn't have borne to have a word said against the puppy he had chosen by instinct rather than skill.

Whatever it was that possessed him, he wouldn't have said it was love for that was a word outside his vocabulary. He just felt what he felt and the wind seemed less bitter and the sun brighter because of it.

Grip

Dudley was to call the puppy Grip, though it took him a while to decide on this name. At first in the boy's opinion he was too small to be given any name at all, too unproved in character. A name had to indicate in some way what the dog was, and so in the beginning he called him 'lad' if he felt the need to call him anything at all.

Daily he would take him out across the moors or through the woods regardless of the weather, wanting to make his muscles strong, determined to make him tough. In the wood he would pick up fallen branches to throw which the puppy raced after with the wildest of joy. Once he got hold of a branch Dudley couldn't get it away from him. He had a mouth like an iron clamp and when his teeth were well into the wood nothing would make him let go.

Many a time Dudley swung the branch in a wide arc round his body and the puppy would go swinging round at the end of it, flying through the air with outstretched

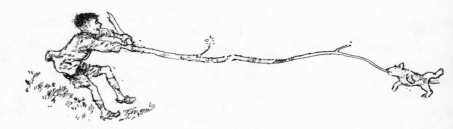

legs and tail but never letting go. Dudley sometimes fell over, ground and sky hitting against each other until he could resist no longer, and when he crawled back on his feet again, head still rocking, the puppy would be waiting for him with the branch hanging from his jaws, tail wagging, eyes gleaming, sometimes looking a bit rocky and dizzy himself, but never letting go. That was why Dudley called him Grip and, as the months went by, he was unable to compete against his strength.

Many a tug-of-war did they have, with an old shoe, a length of tow-rope, a cast-off jacket, and once an umbrella between them, and Dudley tried all the tricks he could think of to win. He would blow hard into Grip's eyes and nose to disconcert and harry him, pull his tail, grab his legs, beat him over the head, but Grip only growled the more fiercely and held on the more determinedly and, in the end, he would proudly carry home his spoil, Dudley following exhausted in his wake.

Grip grew quickly on his diet of porridge, raw eggs and rabbit meat. He was to be a handsomer dog than his sire, with straighter back and more perfect head, but while he was small it was difficult to foretell how he was going to end up because all the different parts of him were out of proportion; one bit seeming to do a bit of growing and then leaving off to let another bit try to catch up. Thus at one period he seemed to be all ears, at another time his body seemed huge and his legs underdeveloped, and his upper jaw much longer than his lower one. By the time he was a year old everything had more or less caught up and his pure white coat glistened with health, showing off the strength of the bone beneath. He wasn't as tall as his sire, nor as heavy, and there was a gentler expression in his small slanted black eyes, with none of the wickedness that gleamed in Madman's.

There was as much stubbornness in him as in any other

dog of his breed and this showed very early in puppy-hood. Sometimes that stubbornness looked more like lack of intelligence because it went hand in hand with a disregard for pain or punishment. It wasn't easy for Dudley to teach his dog obedience. Grip had a way of ignoring every command when he wasn't in a mood to obey. He wanted only to play and be free and in the first months he wrecked the vegetable garden, crashed his way through the wiring of the rabbit pen half a dozen times and got lost on several occasions.

He would be cuffed and kicked for his waywardness and he listened with flattened ears and doleful eyes while Dudley raged at him and perhaps hit him in the face with every cross word, but the minute he felt sure that the boy's anger had subsided his eyes would be sparkling again and he would dance and leap all round him. This was usually enough for Dudley to forgive him but sometimes, if he was exceedingly cross, Grip would slink along beside him and find as many opportunities as possible to lick his fingers, not fawning, just wanting the boy to know that he held no grudge against him.

It was important for Grip to learn obedience. He wasn't just a pet dog, but a powerful animal of a wayward nature and if Dudley couldn't control him there would be no hope of presenting him in the pit when he was older. A well-trained fighting dog, even in the heat of battle, would allow his master to disentangle him from a fight without biting him in his excitement, and he had to have implicit faith in his master's orders as well as instant obedience to them.

Dudley spent hours teaching the puppy to sit, to come, to go, to sit again, to stay. Many a day he neglected to go to school. When the sun shone and the wind from the moor came fresh-scented down to the garden it was hard to pick up his books with the homework he hadn't done and make the three-mile trek down to the school, especially when Grip would look at him with a question in his dark eyes, his whole body trembling with eagerness to explore those scents.

Sometimes it was Grip's fault if he didn't go to school. He would leave the dog shut up in the scullery and set out sullenly, books under his arm, determined to brave out the caning he knew would be waiting for him, and before he had gone very far Grip would have found a way out, either jumping through the open window or nosing up the latch on the door, barking with eagerness as he raced to catch him up. Then Dudley would either have to take him back home and be late for school – which would mean an extra caning – or abandon the idea of school altogether for that day. It was far more agreeable to do the latter and, in order to escape his father's wrath, they would go through the woods and out on to the moor together, spending the whole day there, hunting for rabbits or badger sets or finding shelter against the rain which might suddenly pour down on them, waiting for the sky to tell them that it must be about time to go home.

Bill Kershaw didn't really care about his son getting an education. He knew the boy learned next to nothing at school and, but for the law, wouldn't have sent him. He could read and write and understand plain arithmetic. What more did a lad need to earn his living at the local mills? Now and then an inspector would come up to The Craggs inn with threats of fines or imprisonment for the father, while Dudley himself had to endure the wrath of a headmaster who was determined to 'bring him to heel', as he often put it, and looked for every opportunity to make an example of him.

Dudley never complained to his father about the canings or the hours he spent just standing alone in the school hall, missing most of his lessons even though he was at school. He would shove his swollen, stinging fingers into his trouser pockets and think of Grip; what he intended to teach him next, how to get him out of that last bad habit he had developed; or just remembering the things they did together. Sometimes the headmaster might catch him with an involuntary smile and harshly accuse him of insolence, but Dudley would lower his eyes and stare at his clogs and shut the man out of his world.

Before having the puppy Dudley made an effort to go to school, if only to escape his father's cuffs for not going, but when Grip came into his life it became harder and harder for him. The only thing that interested him was the dog.

To start with, having Grip brought him closer to his father's world of fighting dogs and gave them something to talk about to each other. Bill Kershaw hardly opened his mouth except when in the company of men of his own kind and now his son was part of that world because he had a dog of his own. He had gone with his father to all the fights for as long as he could remember but he had always been an outsider, a hanger-on, useful for keeping an eye open for the police or uninvited strangers, not really part of that secret circle until now.

The dog's training became all important, but it was as hard for Dudley to be constant as it was for Grip. They would go out together, far away from the inn, far away from everything, the dog racing hither and thither, Dudley coming along behind him planning the day's schedule, but the slightest thing could make them both forget what they had gone for. In the summer days, when bees buzzed in the yellow-flowering gorse bushes and swards of heather and there wasn't a shadow across all the moor, they would often flop down together, Dudley to watch the occasional cloud rush across the sky in front of the wind, Grip to watch his master's face and drip saliva over him, and hours would pass before Dudley remembered why he had gone there. Dudley's school day had passed and so had Grip's and many a time they had done nothing but chase each other and sleepily watch the clouds.

Even when it rained Dudley preferred to be out over the moor with his dog. His life had been always so empty of everything, purpose, comfort, affection; a routine of waking, eating, enduring the hours at school to arrive at the end of the day and his unmade bed in the cold, barren room under the eaves of the old stone inn; that this sudden filling of it with everything was almost too over-whelming to be borne.

He had to escape to the moors where he could shout and run about as he had never wanted to do before, his whole body filled with an energy and eagerness that was almost unknown to him. He couldn't have said what it was that possessed him, this feeling in his heart which until now had been as dark and unstirred as an abandoned badger's set, but he knew that he only felt like this because of Grip.

One Sunday in August

One of Dudley's greatest responsibilities was to ensure that Grip and Madman were never alone together. Even while Grip was only a puppy Madman would have torn him apart without any scruple had not his master been around to prevent him.

The problem wasn't so much keeping Madman away from the puppy, but the reverse. Madman was nearly always at Bill Kershaw's side, following him down to the cellar and about the house and garden, watching from a corner while he scrubbed the stone flagged bar, curled up behind the counter while his master served customers of an evening, sharing his bed at night. Wherever Bill Kershaw went, Madman padded along behind him, seeming to notice nothing but his master.

Grip, however, knew nothing of Madman's nature and, feeling the lack of his brothers and sisters, wanted to play with him. The first ten days or so were a nightmare to Dudley. Whenever Madman came into sight Grip would go dashing after him and it was only Bill Kershaw's stern commands that kept the dog from turning on him. He would growl the most ferocious warnings, at which Grip would flatten to the ground for a second, then, seeing the dog trotting off about his business again, he would go charging after him, perhaps trying to catch his tail, yapping insolently. Dudley would yell for him to stay, grabbing at his tail or a leg, the very violence of his command causing the puppy to cringe back in obedience to it. The look in Madman's eyes when the puppy was so close to him sent shudders through Dudley. But how well trained he was! And the boy would realize yet again the importance of teaching Grip the same high standard of control.

'If Madman goes for him,' his father warned, 'there'll be no more puppies for thee.'

It was only by dint of much punishment and scolding that Grip learned to leave Madman alone but the longing to attack him was there. It wasn't a bad feeling on the pup's part, just high spirits. For him the best way of enjoying himself was by testing the strength that was in him, jaws and legs and body, and he and Dudley would wrestle on the floor together, rolling over and over, the boy hitting with hands and knees as hard as he could to defend himself, Grip pummelling with his nose, grabbing with his teeth which, for all his excitement, he controlled so well that he rarely gave the boy more than a nip when he could have bitten deeply into his flesh.

While Dudley was at school his father took over the responsibility of keeping the two dogs apart. Most of the time Grip would be shut up in Dudley's bedroom but he early on learned the trick of nosing up the latch to get out and he would appear unexpectedly, ears cocked, tail wagging, an almost smug expression in his eyes. Then he would be tied up somewhere but, even as he cursed him, Bill Kershaw admired his spirit. It was a good sign.

In spite of the care that both Dudley and his father took to keep the two dogs away from each other, Grip's high-spirited stubbornness was to defeat their efforts. Grip was about seven months old at the time and although he still had much of the gangling youngster about him was beginning to show a greater sense of responsibility as a result of his young master's constant schooling. Both dogs were used to sharing a room by now, Grip at one side of the table, beside Dudley's chair, Madman usually stretched out in front of the kitchen range on the only bit of rug the house possessed.

Madman ignored the younger dog as long as Grip kept out of his way because he knew that this was what was expected of him. He wasn't as jealous of Grip as he had been of previous dogs in his domain because he knew his master cared nothing for him. Had it been otherwise, not even he could have kept him from vengeance. Grip was learning to control his eager heart. However, there were days when he completely forgot all the things Dudley had been teaching him, when all his puppyhood joy rushed over him again, and it was on one of these days that the event so carefully avoided occurred.

It was on a Sunday in August, a rare day of such perfect weather that even the chapel bells seemed to be extolling the morning rather than calling worshippers to prayer; a day when men and women confined for so many hours during the week to the noise and sweat of the woollen mills suddenly sensed a need to feel the sun on their face and recalled the pleasure of paddling their feet in a rushing stream. That Sunday morning Bill Kershaw took one thoughtful look at the promising dawn and knew that there would be good business.

After breakfast, while he brought up extra crates of lemonade from the cellar and dragged them out to the garden, Dudley was busy setting out the trestle tables and chairs which were kept folded up in an outhouse. He had to wash them over to get off the cobwebs and needed several buckets of water to do the job properly. His father knew people would be arriving early and, with a thirst induced by walking along the hot macadam road, few of them would be able to resist the bottles of orange, lemon or lime set out invitingly, almost under their noses as they came past the inn, especially the children. When it looked as though Dudley had finished with the tables and chairs, he sent him to fill their biggest kettle with water and set it over the fire. Most of the women would be asking for a good cup of tea, he knew, and it was as well to be prepared for them, too.

With all this rushing to and fro neither of them thought much about the dogs. Madman, after being cursed out of his master's way a couple of times, stretched himself out beside the inn door, getting the best of the sunshine, while Grip tussled with the piles of dirty chairs and twice ran off with the cloth Dudley was using to wash them.

It was while Dudley was in the scullery, straining his arms under the weight of the heavy kettle which he held to the tap, that Grip, looking for mischief of one kind or another, came upon the dozing, sun-warmed Madman who, for once, was unaware of his approach. All previous training forgotten, he pounced with delight on to the other's flank.

In a flash, as Madman sprang over him, he instinctively understood his peril and only the most basic instinct of all – fear for survival – saved him. His body turned several swift somersaults along the ground, under Madman's feet almost, as he yammered out his utter terror in a hysterical flood of sound. He was a whelp again, claiming the young animal's right to protection, and for a split second Madman hesitated. That pause was just enough for Grip. Springing to all fours, he fled across the road, tail between his legs, still yelping out his fear as Madman pursued him.

Dudley, on hearing the fear-crazed cries, just dropped the kettle into the sink and dashed out. His father was ahead of him and his first wave of fear subsided when he saw that Grip had managed to elude Madman's teeth.

But along with relief went a twinge of pained surprise to see how he fled, making no effort to defend himself.

Madman halted at his master's command and turned back, but Grip went on running, deaf to Dudley's cries, and was out of sight before the other dog was beside Bill Kershaw again.

'Looks more like a greyhound than a fighting dog,' was his father's only comment as he returned to the garden, but Dudley saw the jeering light in his eyes.

Grip didn't return until several hours had passed and when he came back he was very subdued, not that Dudley took much notice of him for he was too busy serving the rush of customers. By the time he was free Grip was wagging his tail again, his eyes as bright as ever, and Dudley had forgotten his flash of disappointment.

Both Dudley and his father had little imagination and neither of them knew how much the morning's incident had affected Grip. They saw that from then on he gave Madman a wide berth but they never guessed that that moment of terror was to affect him as a permanent experience, one of the memory patterns of existence.

Rivalry

From the day that Grip ran away from his first encounter Dudley knew that his father was waiting for the dog to prove himself. He had lost a great deal of merit on that occasion for, although not even his father would have expected the dog to put up much of a fight, they had both expected that he would have tried to defend himself.

Dudley was goaded by the unspoken contempt he had seen in his father's eyes whose estimation, once lost, was difficult to regain. Dudley knew that, because of this incident, one day there would have to be a proper confrontation between Madman and Grip, not a private set to but a public one. Bill Kershaw's silent implication was that if Grip were worthless Madman would make short shrift of him on the right occasion, and the sooner the better.

The fact that Grip was his son's dog only increased his resentment. Time and money were being wasted on him. Had it been a dog of his own, he might well have tied a stone round its neck and dumped it in the pool in the woods, where more than one poor-spirited creature had ended its days. However, Grip was Madman's son and, although he got a perverse satisfaction out of trying to undermine his son's confidence in him, he was prepared to suspend judgement. For both boy and dog the experience over the next year or so would either make or break them, and Bill Kershaw had no use for weaklings.

In many ways he and Madman were alike. He shared his dog's ruthless jealousy of any possible rival and whenever he heard of a new dog Madman had to challenge it. He couldn't tolerate the existence of a fighting dog that Madman hadn't faced and beaten, and it was only a matter of time before Dudley understood that his father looked upon Grip as one of Madman's future foes.

Even while he helped the boy build him up, giving advice and the benefit of all his experience, Dudley knew that he only wanted him to be strong and belligerent because he wanted a worthwhile rival for Madman. At first the idea frightened and repelled him. He had seen enough of Madman's blood-lust to dread the very thought of Grip having one day to face it.

Many a time he secretly hoped that some other dog would come up meanwhile that could put an end to Madman's savage career and, if at one time he had disliked the dog, now he began positively to hate him. This hatred showed in his eyes whenever he saw him lying at his father's feet or sitting unconcernedly behind the bar while his father served the few evening customers, his wicked eyes closed, giving him an almost lamb-like appearance.

His father saw and understood his looks and it was from these that the sense of rivalry grew up between them. Bill Kershaw could wait the year or two years Grip needed to reach sufficient maturity and there was an uncompassionate anticipation in his heart for when that day should come.

Dudley knew how his father felt and he knew too that there would be no avoiding the confrontation. He didn't know why he minded so much. After all, he had faith enough in Grip to want to match him in the pit against other dogs. The trouble with Madman was that his contests were nearly always to the death. A man had to be prepared to lose his dog when he matched it against that savage and this was something Dudley could not contemplate. Grip was everything to him, from the time he first ran his inexperienced hands over him in Joe Barnes' cottage, and whether he became a champion pit dog or not was of secondary importance.

However, there was the unspoken accusation that was hard to ignore and the biggest slight of all to any dog worth its salt. Cowardice! To have a cowardly dog was the worst disgrace its owner could have to face. Better to have it torn to pieces, dying bravely, than turning tail or refusing to come up to scratch. When Dudley understood that his father was determined to see how Grip faced up to Madman one day he had to decide that, when that day came, Grip would either have to win the fight or die. There was no way of getting out of it.

So the unspoken challenge and its acceptance underlay everything that the boy and his dog enjoyed. It was the shadow behind all their walks and exercises, that tempered their association and determined Dudley to make his dog as tough and as hard as he could.

Few dogs fought before they were a year old and, even then, a man who wanted to bring his dog on to higher things wouldn't overwork him. Dudley was certain that his father wouldn't expect Grip to face Madman before he was a two-year-old at least and by then Madman himself would be older, perhaps not so swift though probably a good bit meaner to make up for it.

From hoping that another dog would cripple or kill him in the meantime, Dudley almost began to wish that Madman would keep his full strength and so remain a worthwhile challenge. Because of one thing he was sure. Grip was going to be the best one day, better even than his sire. As far as he was concerned Madman had already met his match. One day his own son would vanquish him.

Not too much time went by before Grip at last had a real chance to show something of his spirit and this was at a badger-baiting organized by Bill Kershaw when someone brought him a badger he had trapped. The animal was put in the cellar of The Crags inn where it was left to recover from its ordeal in a large, stout box which had been used for this purpose before. The top of the box was covered with wire netting.

Dudley was fascinated by the captive which demonstrated an aggressiveness equal to anything he had ever seen in a dog. It was a huge animal, a good three feet long from the tip of its snout to the end of its tail, and there was a tremendous amount of weight in its thickset body. Dudley thought it would be difficult for any dog to get a valid grip through its thick hair, and the teeth he had seen, together with the swiftness of its movements in spite of its heaviness, made him realize that any dog faced with such a creature would be fighting for its life.

Word went round among those men who had dogs of the right kind interested in the entertainment, and the chance of a bit of cheap excitement together with the hope of winning a few shillings was hard to resist. Thus on the night of the baiting the bar was fuller than it had been for many a day and most of its occupants had dogs of one kind or another at their heels. Terriers large and small, good ratters most of them and of undisputed courage, as well as dogs of Madman's breed and the odd mongrel.

In the meantime Bill Kershaw had used boards to construct a ten-foot tunnel down in the cellar, wired over, which connected to the badger's box. The idea was that the dogs should take it in turn to run along this tunnel, grab the badger and try to drag him out. The one who first succeeded, if any did, would be declared champion but because there were so many dogs they were initially to be given three minutes each at the badger, each man paying for his dog's turn as well as laying on any bets that might appeal to him. The inscription fee would go to the champion at the end of the evening.

When everything was ready and lots had been drawn for the order in which the dogs should be set at the badger, Bill Kershaw locked the door of the public bar and led the way down to the cellar.

Badger

The badger already seemed to sense what was awaiting him. He was pressed well into the corner of his box, facing the opening that led to the tunnel but not adventuring into it in search of escape, feeling safer in the prison he already knew. The men crowded as close to the tunnel as they could, their hard, dour faces alight with excitement, each man clinging to his dog to prevent it from jumping on to the wire in eagerness to get at the badger.

Dog after dog took it in turn to rush along the tunnel, encouraged by yells and shouts, to be met each time by the bared fangs of the thirty-pound badger who moved his head with snake-like swiftness and ripped with the sharpness of a wolf. The badger was heavier than half the dogs that confronted him and, though there was much growling and yapping and teeth that met flesh, none of them managed to drag the badger out of his box.

As Grip's turn got closer and still the badger seemed to have more energy in him than any of the dogs that had been set on him so far, Dudley found himself shivering with uneasiness. At the same time, sweat was soaking through his jersey. Grip was going to have to go down that tunnel and risk getting his nose torn off without retreating in order to prove that he had the guts required of him. He wanted his turn to come quickly now. He wanted him to get it over. He didn't care whether he

managed to drag the badger out or not, as long as he
didn't show fear.

He shot a glance at his father who was surveying the
proceedings from behind the badger's box, Madman
beside him, his jaws stretched in a wide grin of anticipation. Saliva from them dripped on to the badger's
ruffled coat but Madman wasn't watching the badger. He
had eyes only for the other dogs and Dudley could tell by
his expression that he would have taken on each one of
them in turn that night to satisfy his lust.

Bill Kershaw saw the boy's glance. He gave a mocking look at Grip who had his paws up on the tunnel wall, ears pricked, then yelled out to the crowd, 'Ten to one Grip can get that badger halfway along the tunnel.'

There was a loud outcry among the sportsmen. Ten to one on an untried dog! Grip became the centre of everyone's attention. Before bets were finally settled an argument ensued as to what was exactly 'halfway along the tunnel', and so a line was drawn in chalk on the boards, denoting the point to which the dog must draw the badger in order that Bill Kershaw should win his bet.

Dudley hated him just then. He was only doing it to mock him, not because he had that much faith in Grip.

By now the badger was tiring. He had fought off eleven dogs already and his head and shoulders were covered with blood, whether his own or that of his opponents was difficult to say. For the first time that night silence almost fell over the heavily-breathing mass of men and dogs as Dudley brought Grip to the tunnel entrance and faced him down it. As had done the other dogs before him, Grip rushed to the badger's box and poked his head through the opening, tail wagging. He was eager for a game, Dudley knew.

The badger looked up at this new face. In the beginning he had slashed at every nose as it appeared but now he was huddled up in a corner. He would defend himself still but was no longer prepared to attack. The ears were flat, the eyes were baleful, the teeth still bared.

Grip went on wagging his tail, half in, half out of the box, and the silence continued while everyone waited to see what would happen next. Dudley was in agony at the other end of the tunnel, fists clenched, teeth biting his lower lip. A loud bark broke from Grip. He wanted the badger to play with him! Laughter started somewhere among the men and it grew louder as Grip went on barking and wagging his tail.

'Minute gone,' reminded someone.

'Get him, Grip,' cried Dudley desperately. 'Get him.'

Grip was disconcerted. He sensed the animosity of the cornered animal, the smell of fear and hate, and realized that this wasn't a game after all. The badger wasn't there to be played with; didn't want to play. And then there was his master, urging him on, giving him an order.

One of his favourite games with the boy was bringing him things, from the time when the first sticks were thrown for him as a two-month puppy through to the increasingly difficult tasks that were set. Dudley would wedge the sticks between rocks on the moor or hide them in almost inaccessible places and if Grip didn't or couldn't bring them back he knew he was in trouble. His reward for success was his master's delight. However, he had never been asked to get him a living creature before and the order puzzled him.

He pulled his head out of the box and raced back to Dudley amid jeers, boos and laughter from the spectators. The boy, red-faced, furious and ashamed, met him with a kick which sent him down the tunnel again towards the badger.

'Get him,' he ordered for the third time, his voice hoarse with emotion.

There was a lot of bantering about Bill Kershaw's bet but it began to die down as for the second time Grip poked his head into the box. This time it looked as though he meant business but he was still very cautious about it and wasting valuable time.

The badger sensed Grip's indecision. Canny animal that he was, the experience of the evening had shown him that attack invited attack. He was weary of the baiting and wanted to be left in peace in his corner.

Whining now, anxious to please his master but not sure how to go about it, Grip made a tentative lunge which the badger ignored. He sniffed at the bloody black and white head and the badger drew even closer into himself, refusing to be drawn. Grip's tail began to wave again. His confidence was growing. This time he nudged quite fiercely at the badger's flank, looking for a place to take hold.

'Two minutes,' yelled the timekeeper.

It was then that the badger struck, one flashing movement that ripped along the jaw. Grip's reaction was to sink his teeth into the badger's flank and start dragging with all his might to get the creature back to his master as he was commanded.

He had chosen a bad place to take hold because the badger had all the freedom of his head and forequarters with which to defend himself, but now that Grip had him he wasn't letting go. Again and again the badger slashed at him and Grip became frantic to complete his task, dragging backwards with all his strength, forcing the badger along the tunnel although he fought him all the way.

The men were almost hysterical with excitement. It was the best battle of the evening and although time was fast running out for Grip so were those solid legs of his gradually inching back towards the line that had been chalked on the boards. The badger alternated now between trying to drag himself back to his quarters and attempting to tear himself free from the dog's jowls, and he used both teeth and claws on his attacker's body, inflicting terrible punishment.

But Grip hadn't earned his name lightly. With eyes shut tight he went on pulling, pulling, hearing the boy's encouraging, commanding voice, ignoring the pain. The badger was across the line and a spontaneous cheer broke from the spectators, but still Grip wouldn't let go. Not until the badger was almost at Dudley's feet did he look up, as if to ask if the boy were satisfied, and the order to let go was given.

The badger crawled back to his box as soon as he felt himself released and for a while he was forgotten as the men crowded round Dudley and his dog, congratulating them both.

Dudley enjoyed the pride of that moment, even while the cause of it sat trembling with effort at his feet, panting and bleeding. When the excitement was over and still another dog was set to the draw, Dudley took Grip back to the kitchen where he warmed up some water in the kettle to clean his wounds, then paint them with iodine, rewarding him in his own way with words of pleasure and caressing hands.

Judgement

Although Dudley was well satisfied with Grip's performance at the badger-baiting his father was not. True he had nigh on killed it but he had shown none of the pugnaciousness so necessary to the character of a successful fighting dog.

Weighing up Grip's performance the following morning over breakfast, Bill Kershaw said thoughtfully, 'If tha hadn't ordered him on, if tha hadn't taught him to fetch, happen Grip would never have touched that badger.'

'He did more than any other dog last night,' defended Dudley.

'Aye, I'll not say he didn't, but his heart wasn't in it, and a dog without heart is no good in a fight.'

'It was his first try,' argued Dudley. 'He didn't know what he had to do.'

'That's just it. He should've known. He should've felt it. Instinct is what he lacks. Instinct. If he hasn't got the instinct you might as well be rid of him. He'll never do nowt in the pit.'

There was nothing Dudley could answer to this. He could only wait until the time came for Grip to prove himself. He was old enough now for a fight to be arranged for him but first he would have to recover from his wounds which were severe.

Grip had eaten no porridge that morning, too sick to do

so. His whole body was fevered. Dudley had felt the un-
natural heat of it as soon as he had woken that day, for
Grip shared his bed and gave him more warmth than the
blankets in the ice-cold room could ever do. Although
there was a fireplace in the room it was hardly ever used.
Bill Kershaw had little money to spare for coal and the inn,
with its stone walls under the slate roof and the shadow of
the crags over it, was cold even in midsummer. A fire was
kept going in the kitchen, beside which they always sat,
and that morning Dudley had pulled his blankets off the
bed and taken them downstairs for Grip to lie on in front
of the fire.

He had had to half carry, half drag the dog downstairs
because Grip could hardly walk, weak with the heat that
was in him as well as the stiffness from his wounds. The
badger had torn chunks out of his left shoulder, as well as

splitting his ear and slashing his neck and jaw, and perhaps Dudley hadn't been as thorough with the cleansing of the wounds as he ought to have been. Whatever the reason, pus had formed in the deeper wounds overnight and Grip was languishing.

Dudley had been awake before his father, before the break of day, and he had made up the fire himself, oppressed with fear for the dog's well-being. He had seen Madman with wounds which his father had treated with salt water and iodine, as he had done the night before with Grip, but Madman seemed invincible even in this. His injuries always healed rapidly and without any bother. He had sat beside Grip, pulling the blankets up round him, stroking his broad head softly and telling him not to worry, that soon he would be champion again. But Grip hadn't even acknowledged his presence; nose on paws, dry, rough and hot; eyes shut tight; and he didn't seem even half the dog he had been the day before.

When Bill Kershaw came down, Madman at his heels as usual, and saw the state of him, he shut his own dog out of the kitchen and gave Grip a thorough looking-over. He opened the festering wounds and cleansed them with peroxide which formed frothy bubbles over the jagged flesh.

'Tha'll have to do that two or three times a day until the flesh is clean,' he told Dudley.

He brought out some rolls of old sheeting which had long ago been torn into strips for bandages and covered the worst wounds with them as best he could. Even while he watched all his father did for the dog with expert hands, Dudley sensed the contempt he felt for Grip, as if he knew he was wasting his time.

More than a month went by before Grip recovered fully from his encounter with the badger and his left ear never stood up straight again afterwards. Bill Kershaw curtly reminded his son that he should have cropped his ears anyway as they were the most vulnerable part of his body but Dudley remembered, even though he had been very small at the time, how much Madman had suffered at his ear-cropping and wouldn't agree to it.

'Tha's soft,' jeered his father, 'and that dog of thine is soft, too.'

'He isn't. He isn't,' retorted Dudley, deeply stung but refusing to be goaded into giving way. 'He'll kill Madman one day, just see if he doesn't.'

'He'll end up in the river if he doesn't do summat worth while soon.'

'He's my dog and he'll never end up in the river.'

'Thee'll be the one that chucks him there.'

The only way to avoid his father's bantering was by pretending not to care. Dudley never had cared until now how harsh his father might be with him. It was only his affection for Grip that had made his heart less callous, less indifferent. He was twelve years old but until he had felt the softness of a dog's tongue on his fingers there had been no gentleness in his life.

Thinking about his father's accusation, he wondered if it was true. Perhaps Grip was making him soft. The possibility frightened and angered him. He told himself he would be hard and so would Grip and between them they would vanquish all who believed otherwise.

Grip versus *Jack*

There had been a time, before the law was changed, when dog fighting had been considered an honourable sport, with 'Articles of Agreement' which were drawn up between the owners of the dogs and witnessed by several people. These Articles not only gave the exact date and hour of the fight but also the weight of each dog, the amounts of money involved, and the rules to be followed. When dog fighting was outlawed nobody was any longer prepared to sign a document that could be used against him in evidence, but the Articles still stood, to be honoured by a handshake once agreed upon.

The rules were as strict as any that had ever been drawn up for prize-fighters. Each dog had his corner and a second to look after him, and the fight was divided into rounds, a round ending either when both dogs had gone away from each other or had made a mutual pause for rest. They could then be retrieved by their seconds and revived in their corners for the next round, and there was both a timekeeper and a referee to ensure that fair play was observed.

Pits where the dogs fought were no longer in existence but this did not deter the men who clung to the outlawed sport. Barns, pub cellars or open countryside were equally satisfactory and many precautions were taken to ensure that no one outside their circle should come upon them.

46

The actual site of the engagement was determined only the night before the contest at the toss of a coin.

There was a place on the moors that was Bill Kershaw's favourite, a small, natural amphitheatre which couldn't have been bettered by man. To start with it was a long way from the nearest lonely cottage, where only wandering sheep left prints in the peat and were sometimes sucked down, bleating and helpless, into bogs. There were no trees, walls or footpaths and the spectators who sat on the slopes about this small, grass-covered circle had a first-class view of the proceedings as well as an uninterrupted vision of the moorland on every side of them. The law couldn't creep up on them unawares while, approaching from a distance, the spectators could be seen but not what engaged their attention. Should the police or other un-welcome intruders turn up, the meeting suddenly became a dog-fanciers' club, the scratch-line marked off in peat part of the innocent judging ring. It was well-organized. However, with a three-month prison sentence or a heavy fine to threaten them, even this place wasn't used fre-quently. Caution was more important than comfort.

It was here that Grip was to make his first appearance as a fighting dog. His exploit with the badger had been spoken of in all the local dog fighting circles and there were several who wanted to test his mettle but as Dudley, his owner, was only a boy Bill Kershaw had to make the arrangements for him. However, they went together and although Dudley didn't do any of the talking, he sat in the other man's living room one evening, insignificant among the half-dozen men gathered there but a keen listener.

When Dudley saw his father take the ten-pound deposit money out of his pocket he turned his head away, pre-ferring not to see any glance that might be thrown at him. If Grip won, the twenty pounds, plus any extra bets that

47

his father might choose to lay on the day, was a small fortune. If he lost . . . But he wasn't going to lose, and most of the money his father was laying out that night had been gained at the badger-baiting anyway.

The fight was to take place on the following Sunday morning at the earliest possible hour, long before the men had to join their wives and families in chapel for the morning service. Five o'clock was fixed upon. They expected the fight to last half an hour or more, and there was talk of matching another pair of dogs for the same day.

Dawn broke just after four that Sunday morning, but both Dudley and his father were up much earlier, to be on their way to the meeting place before the sun began to loom up as a red mist over the horizon. The moor was still almost dark at that hour and they had to be careful where they trod. Thick mist clung in pockets, concealing whole stretches of land, making it look to Dudley as though there was nothing beyond where they set their feet, as though they were approaching emptiness.

As the sun came up there was a burst of bird song high above their heads. Dudley and the dogs automatically looked up but they could see nothing except yellow fire touching the rims of clouds, fading into blueness. His father had heard skylarks many a time and was unimpressed by them. It was more important to watch the ground.

They met up with others travelling in the same direction and Dudley fell behind with Grip, not wanting to talk to anyone, wishing neither to boast nor defend. All too soon Grip would be showing those who wanted to know what he was made of. No words of Dudley's could be as explicit as that.

Even though he had the highest faith in Grip's potential he couldn't help the feeling of anxiety that leaped in his stomach. So much depended on today. His father had encouraged him to feed him up the last few days to see if he could get another pound of weight on to him. Now that his first combat was within sight even he was anxious for Grip to have every advantage. Dudley knew that it wasn't for the money. His father was a fair man. Precisely because he had no faith in him he wanted to be sure that Grip's chances were even.

And they were. When Dudley saw the two dogs together he could find no obvious difference between them. They could have been brothers of the same litter if size had anything to do with it. Grip betrayed his youth in the eagerness with which he surveyed his surroundings, tail wagging, eyes bright. The other dog, Jack, was calmer but there was an equal brightness about him.

The scratch line was set in peat across the centre of the ring and stones were piled up to denote the opposing corners. It wasn't considered necessary to taste either dog. Bill Kershaw was too well known to be believed capable of such nobbling tricks as applying mustard or vinegar to the dog's coat and so was Jack's master. Dudley was allowed in the ring to look after his dog and the referee explained the rules carefully to him. He'd seen the boy around at enough turn-ups to believe that he knew as much about the rules as did his father. Still, it was his job to make sure.

Dudley went to his corner with Grip and took off his jacket. There was a bucket of water there with a cloth for sponging the dog down between rounds. Grip was thirsty and began lapping at it but Dudley dragged him away. If he filled himself up with water before starting he'd be no good for anything.

Jack watched Grip from the other corner. Although not very experienced he knew what this morning's affair was all about and was eager to get to it. Dudley could hear

him whining. His whines drew Grip's attention. He pricked his good ear, his whole body quivering.

'Bonnie lad,' whispered Dudley encouragingly, bending to massage Grip's heavy shoulders. His father always did this with Madman, reckoning that even while it stimulated his spirit it calmed his nerves. Dudley didn't know if it would make any difference to Grip, who went on wagging his tail and grinning, but having something to do while he waited definitely helped him. 'Make mincemeat of that Jack,' he told him. 'Make mincemeat of him.'

At last the referee called them up to the scratch line and the crowd fell silent as the two dogs sniffed each other's noses, still restrained by their masters. The timekeeper yelled 'Let go!' just as Jack uttered a strangled growl, lungeing at Grip even before his leash was removed.

Collars were off; the seconds were away; Jack flew straight for Grip's head. And Grip, faced by an onslaught as ferocious and unexpected as had been that of Madman in his youth, reacted in the same panic-stricken way that had saved him then. He fled, tail between legs, his whole body an expression of terror. In vain Dudley called to him. He was out of the circle and away over the moor, while the spectators jeered and booed, cursed or laughed, according to how they had laid their bets.

Nothing had made Dudley cry since he was a toddler, since before he could even remember, but that morning, such was his disappointment, such was his rage and disbelief, that his eyes were blurred with tears. He struggled for breath, feeling his dog's desertion as a fierce blow on the chest, unaware of the scornful noises all about him, his heart cramped with pain.

The dog-baiting

Grip had been Dudley's dog for more than a year and as a companion there was nothing to beat him. Before Grip came into his life and gave it purpose and joy, Dudley had never known that such happiness could exist. Taming that unruly spirit, as gay as it was stubborn, had taught him that life wasn't only composed of hardness, coldness and emptiness. There was the love that glowed in his dog's eyes whenever Dudley happened to look at him; that rippled through every delighted contortion of his body when they went off together through the woods or across the moor; that was in the moist tongue caressing his fingers of a night-time when he stirred from sleep and automatically searched for his dog's head.

It was the knowledge of all this that Dudley struggled with as he tramped home, lowering his head against the wind that sighed and moaned as if unaware of the brilliant sunshine. Grip was coming along somewhere behind him. He didn't care where. He didn't look back or once call to him.

Bill Kershaw had stayed behind to watch the second match and perhaps recover some of his lost deposit. Dudley hadn't been able to face him. He wanted to be alone, completely alone. He couldn't even bear Grip's company just then, especially not Grip's, but all the time he was aware that the dog shadowed him – fully conscious of his disgrace if not the reason for it – and his heart cried out against him. He still struggled with a pain that was too hard to be borne, forcing tears that the wind was quick to dry on his face. If Grip had come close to him then the chances were that he would have given him much more punishment than Jack would ever have inflicted, and Grip would have stood there and taken it because Dudley was his god.

What did you do with a fighting dog that wouldn't fight? Dudley knew the answer to that as well as anyone. You tied a rope round its neck if it was too big to go in a sack, you fastened a heavy stone to the rope and you threw both into the canal or the pond. The river wasn't deep enough. Its waters were swift but they wouldn't drown a dog, not at The Crags anyway.

It was a physical struggle for Dudley to admit the words that hammered in his whole being. Grip was a coward. He had run away from Madman once and now he had run away from Jack, without even trying to defend himself. His only instinct had been to run, as if he were any common old mongrel to be found on any street corner. Coward. Coward. The very pain it caused him gave Dudley satisfaction. It helped him to overcome the disgust he felt with himself for loving such a dog.

He had thought that the battle with the badger had proved something but now he knew that it hadn't. It only showed that Grip was obedient to him, would die for him if necessary or endure any amount of pain. Grip hadn't been brave that night. He had only been obedient. He would never have touched the badger if his master hadn't commanded it of him.

But dog fights were different. You couldn't make your dog fight another. He had to want to. Just having another dog presented to him had to be enough for him to want to beat it. It wasn't necessary for there to be a quarrel between them. The sole fact that another dog was there was sufficient challenge.

Madman was a killer and the bitch who mothered Grip had fought for more than a year without a defeat, so what had happened to the bold, pig-headed puppy he had chosen? The worst thing of all, the raging agony inside him, was not that Grip hadn't been the first to attack but that he hadn't even defended himself. There was no excuse for his running away and no pardon.

When he got home, Dudley shut himself inside the house, not wanting to know what Grip did or where he was. If Madman came back and found him he only hoped he would tear him to pieces. It was what he deserved. And to think that for so long he had nursed the thought of Grip defeating Madman! He went up to his room and threw himself on his bed, staying there for the rest of the morning and hoping that when his father returned his own rage would be such that he himself would drag Grip down to the pond in the woods and drown him. Dudley never wanted to see him again.

But Bill Kershaw didn't admit defeat so easily. The dog had been in his house for more than a year, eating good food, costing good money. He was young and strong but he had been too much pampered by Dudley's feelings for him. To cure him of his penchant for running away, he decided to stage a dog-baiting with Grip as the victim. Chained to the cellar wall, he would have to defend himself, and while fighting for his life he might perhaps discover the instinct that should have been bred into him.

Dudley wasn't grateful. He had expected his father to rage, he was prepared to accept his contempt, but having to endure his dog's humiliation yet again was unbearable to him. Equally unbearable was having Grip continue to adore him in the days that followed even though he felt his master's scorn. Dudley had hardened his heart against

Grip because loving him was far too painful and he wanted to be rid of him. He banished him from his bed and company, keeping him shut up in an outhouse, and there were no more walks or fondlings. He hated his father for insisting on giving him another chance, certain that he was laughing at them both, but in spite of himself, when the evening of the baiting came round, he couldn't help hoping again.

The men brought their ratters or whatever dogs they possessed and paid Bill Kershaw for the chance of setting them at Grip. One man came with a greyhound which was making a name for itself as a fighter rather than a runner. It won no races but was so vicious that its muzzle was only ever removed for it to eat.

Grip fought that night, unwillingly at first, defending himself, but as dog after dog attacked him – sometimes three at once on all sides, yapping, growling, darting out of his reach, dashing in again – he began to anticipate

their movements and try to get them before they got him. By the time half the dogs had had their go at him there was the look of his sire about him. His eyes glazed like Madman's as the most primitive of all instincts overpowered him.

The mood of the betting changed as Grip's frenzy grew and the men flung dog after dog at him, wondering how long he could resist them. All but the gamest refused to return for a second round, in spite of their master's boots or fists. They knew as well as the men that nothing would halt Grip now. The gamest ones were crippled or killed and when there were none left to challenge him the maddened dog raged at the end of his chain.

Another chance

When it was over, with Grip on the rug before the kitchen grate, huddled in blankets to ward off the chill that could so quickly follow his overheated state – the deadly chill that so often with fighting dogs led to pneumonia and death – the bitterness was gone from Dudley's heart. He lay on the rug beside the dog, raised on one elbow, his free hand slowly stroking the hard white head, and told himself he should have had more faith. He shouldn't have condemned so easily.

After all, Grip was young, inexperienced. He hadn't known what was expected of him in his match with Jack. After tonight he would know. He had learned to fight, learned to kill. When next confronted by an adversary he would have the memory of this evening to serve him. He wouldn't run away again.

'Bonnie lad,' he said softly, time and time again, as if with the words knowing that Grip would understand and forgive his lack of faith in him.

Now and again Grip opened his dark eyes for a moment but he was too exhausted to take more heed than this. From time to time he shivered and Dudley pulled the blankets still closer around him then got up to stoke the fire and throw on a little more coal. If he died now before he had a chance to redeem himself. . . . But he wouldn't. Grip was tough. He would hang on. Wasn't that how he had earned his name in the first place? His torn ear had been remangled in the fray that night and there was many a new gash on his chest and shoulders but for Dudley these were the wounds of a hero and not to be regretted.

His father came in and, after kicking Madman out of the room when he made a sudden lunge at the dog on his rug, put the kettle over the fire to make them a mug of tea. He sat in the tattered armchair beside the stove, over whose arm hung one of Dudley's shirts for airing, and looked down at the boy and his dog, his black eyebrows thoughtfully drawn together.

'What does tha' think?' was Dudley's anxious question after a few minutes of silence.

Bill Kershaw shook his head. 'I don't know,' was all he said just then and he got up to throw the old tea-leaves from the pot over the coals, where their sudden hissing made Grip jerk his head up, startled. Not until the tea was in the mugs and the man back in the armchair did he speak again.

'He's a right funny dog,' he said. 'Can't say as I've ever seen one quite like him before. Neither nowt nor summat, as the saying goes.'

There was silence while he drank from his mug and then he suddenly exclaimed, 'There was a moment when he looked just like Madman as a youngster.'

'But he will fight, won't he?' insisted Dudley, which was all he cared about.

His father shrugged, his enthusiasm gone. 'Nay. Don't count on it. Happen he might and, then again, happen he mightn't.'

The old resentment flooded back to Dudley's heart. 'Tha' doesn't think he's worth it.'

'I've just got eyes in my head, that's all. Aye, he fought all right. I'm not denying that, but it was only because he had to. When they first started coming at him he wanted to run away. That was plain a mile off. That dog doesn't like fighting and if that's the way he feels there's nowt anyone can do about it.'

'But it was only at first. Once he got het up he was all right, wasn't he?'

'Aye, but . . .'

'It was thee who said to give him another chance.'

'Aye, and I have, and I still don't think he'll come up to scratch in the pit. Give him a chance to run and he'll run. I'm telling thee that even though tha doesn't want to believe it.'

Dudley's dark eyes stared implacably into his father's. 'He'll fight next time if tha'll give him the chance.'

'A lot of brass is needed to fix up a fight. Last time I lost it.'

'Tha's won it enough times with Madman. Tha's made some tonight with Grip.'

His father said nothing. He finished his tea and then got up and stretched himself. 'Well, I'm going up to bed.' He went to the door and called his dog.

'What about Grip?' cried Dudley.

'I'll think on it.'

'Give him a chance. He won't run away next time. I know he won't. And if he does . . . if he does, I'll take him myself and drown him.'

A derisive grunt was Bill Kershaw's reply as he switched off the light and shut the door behind him.

It wasn't really dark in the kitchen even though the hands of the mahogany clock on the mantelpiece were nearing midnight. The fire's glow was brighter in the dark and Dudley could see Grip, which was all he wanted to see, as plain as if it were morning. He was tired, weary with the excitement of the evening, but the anger in his heart against his father kept him awake. He still doubted. He still derided.

'But thee'll show him, won't thee?' he said to Grip. 'Thee'll be the best yet.'

Grip sighed. His shivering had stopped. After stroking him a while more, Dudley put his head against the dog's haunch and pulled a loose end of one of the blankets over him. The heat of the fire made his eyes feel heavy. He yawned and was soon asleep.

The next morning Bill Kershaw agreed to give Grip one more chance. Dudley was so delighted that the caning he was given at school that day for being late, for a previous absence and for wearing clogs that splintered the floorboards – four strokes in all – was a minor irritation. He felt so cheerful that day at school that for once he didn't even mind displaying his swollen palms to the morbidly curious, though he was always uncomfortable when any of his classmates talked to him. Their sympathy embarrassed him.

A fight couldn't be fixed until Grip's wounds were sufficiently healed even though Dudley was anxious for it to take place as soon as possible. He would not admit to any doubts but he definitely did not want Grip to have too much time in which to forget his latest experiences. Meanwhile he returned to all his old fondness for him, spending hours in his company, away from home, away from school.

Summer came late to the moor but when it came it was glorious. Only cloud shadows darkened its greenness but these were chased by the winds with such constancy and capriciousness that from minute to minute its aspect changed. The dark was suddenly light, the light dark, and what was yellow now seemed golden, and what was purple turned to pink. Birds squabbled and sang both in the sky and on the ground, but it was the sound of the wind that captured the boy's attention more than anything else. Sometimes, in that wide, uncultivated wilderness, only the wind really seemed to belong there, master of everything.

Perhaps for the townspeople the woods were more beautiful, with the rushing river and its flashes of kingfishers, the lacy ferns and ageless trees, but there was a darkness there, a closing in that didn't exist on the moor. For Dudley, whose days were divided between the almost melancholic discomfort of his home and the crabbed grimness of his school, the moor, the wind and his dog were his only pleasures. With the sun on his face and the breeze in his hair and Grip racing about over the turf, hunting for rabbit burrows or bird nests, Dudley could forget that life held either responsibilities or pain.

Grip versus *Gladiator*

Grip's second contest was with a dog called Gladiator, a white bull terrier with a black patch over his left eye. He was a rough-looking animal whose master cared more about what he could get out of him than what he put into him. Gladiator weighed nine pounds less than Grip although he was taller, but his master was prepared to risk his chances. Grip's behaviour at his first fight was by now common knowledge among all the fanciers and most people were surprised when Bill Kershaw was prepared to back him for a second time. Of course, he had killed three dogs down in the cellar of The Crags inn but a dog-baiting was different and didn't necessarily prove anything.

The fight was to take place in a barn on a Lancashire farm, just over the border. Gladiator's master was a Lancashire man, so that, added to the usual interest, was the rivalry between the two counties which meant that the turn-up would be a popular one. A Yorkshire dog against a Lancashire dog was something to be seen, even though neither dog had quality. The Yorkshire men felt obliged to back Grip, whatever his chances. Some of them stuck white roses in their lapels with which to taunt their foes and there was more hostility between the men than between the dogs.

Had Grip been less of an unknown quantity the men

gathered there that day would have been more prepared to back him than they were. They could count on Gladiator being withdrawn if Grip put up a good fight, but the question in all their minds was – would he?

Because of the doubt and rivalry there was much excitement that morning, with more money being staked than was usual. Dudley had hardly slept the night before, remembering the promise he had made to his father should Grip fail yet again. He wouldn't fail, he knew he wouldn't, but never had there been so much turmoil within him before that day and never before had an eight-mile walk seemed so daunting. His legs felt as weak as his stomach.

When they first set out Grip was happy but his mood changed when they reached the barn where dogs and men were already gathered, their voices loud and hard, the dogs at the heels of those who had brought them strung up and irritable. Dudley understood Grip well enough to know that he was unhappy as soon as he entered the barn, but he refused to be discouraged.

Because of the rivalry between the two factions, it had been agreed that the dogs should be tasted before the fight commenced. At one time a man had been employed to lick the dogs over from head to tail to guarantee their freedom from obnoxious treatments but not any more. In modern terms, the tasting meant washing the dogs from head to tail in the presence of witnesses with milk that had been bought fresh the same morning, also before witnesses. The farmer supplied the milk, which was still warm from one of his cows, and the men had seen it go straight from the udder to the bucket so they knew it was good.

Dudley held Grip still while a man from Gladiator's side washed him over. His father was doing the same with the other dog. There was only a moment when Dudley had his dog entirely to himself, time enough for him to bend down and whisper to him all his hopes.

'Tha's got to do it this time, lad. Tha's got to go out there and win.'

The dogs were brought up to each other at the scratch line, the order to let go was given, and Dudley stepped away with a sense of desperation. The whole of Grip's future would depend on the next few seconds.

Gladiator was a cautious fighter. Instead of flying straight for Grip's head as Jack had done he circled stiffly round him, his thin body swelling till his skin was tight, almost a shell of protection. Grip followed his movements, circling slowly with him, not trying to engage him.

'Go to it, Gladiator,' snarled his owner, just as the dog himself had decided that here was no opponent to respect, and with a triumphant growl he lunged for Grip's stifle.

Grip twisted out of the way before the teeth could close over his flesh but this was enough for him. Once more he was out of the circle like a shot, diving between the spectators and dashing to the end of the barn, where escape was cut off. He ran up and down the length of the wall before finally halting in a corner to glare defiantly at those who would have him fight and who for a second were speechless with surprise.

Gladiator, bewildered by the loss of his opponent, was forgotten as suddenly Madman flashed from amid the crowd and threw himself on Grip. Dudley was never to know whether his father deliberately released him or whether the dog himself took advantage of the moment to settle old jealousies. At the back of the crowd now, which had grown in close around the two dogs, he could see nothing. He could hear the dogs' voices amid the shouts of the men who, quick to turn loss to advantage, cried out new odds on this unexpected battle.

'Odds on Madman'll murder him.'

'Twenty to one he'll get away.'

But even before there were any takers Dudley saw Grip catapult through the crowd once more and make straight for the barn door, which he hadn't seen before. He was gone, leaving a splatter of blood over the straw on the ground and the whole gathering of men in an uproar.

Dudley didn't know how Grip found his way back home but he was there before them, sitting outside the scullery door, head to one side, favouring the ear that had been torn open again. Madman made a lunge at him but his master checked him. He looked at Dudley but didn't need to say anything. All the way back from the Lancashire barn they hadn't spoken to each other. What was there to say? A fight had broken out between two men from opposing counties which made up for the disappointment of the dog fight but the red rose had won that, too, much to the chagrin of all the Yorkshire men who had gone there. Gladiator's master was well content and so was the farmer, who invited them all back another day. Upon Dudley lay the weight of all the shame.

He went for a length of rope which he knew he could find in the cellar, searching for a longish piece since he would need to make more than one loop, and with this in his hands he called to his dog. Grip followed unwillingly, tail flattened and only its tip wagging nervously. He knew.

The pond was on the gloomiest side of the woods where greens seemed turned to greys and russets to ochre dust. The water was still, its edges thick with weed and slime. How it came to be there Dudley didn't know. It was a good way from the river, hedged on one side by dark holly bushes, swarming with gnats, a silent place overshadowed by tall, clinging trees. Dudley had always felt that this

was a sinister place, ever since he had discovered it by
accident years ago, before the time he first saw his father
drown a dog there.

He stood looking at the turbid water, unaware of time.
It was dark, evil-looking, cold, a reflection of much that
was in his heart just then. If he could make the dog disappear from his heart just by having him disappear into

the depths of this still darkness at his feet he would have gladly kept the promise he had made, but even as he stood there in bitter, humiliated contemplation he knew it would serve no purpose. He couldn't rid his heart of Grip by drowning him. He couldn't rid his heart of Grip at all. Perhaps he could have done the deed a few hours back, when the heat of his contempt was at its greatest, but with the dog standing there beside him, knowing, accepting, it was futile to pretend.

Flinging down the rope, he turned away from the pool, making instinctively for the moor, running through the trees, looking for the light and freedom beyond them. Grip followed unbidden but he didn't overtake the boy or jump up at his side as was his custom when they ran together.

When the moor was reached Dudley slowed to a walk and he walked until he could do so no longer, careless of where he put his feet, splashing through rivulets and mud, tripping over stones, trampling the heather, longing for the ever constant wind to blow all feeling from his being, wishing he could be hard and empty again as he had been before Grip had made him soft.

He came to a road and halted. On the other side was a thick grass verge with a stone wall beyond enclosing sloping pasture land where brown cows grazed. Beyond the meadows were the tops of a few trees and beyond them the town, smoke over the black slate roofs diluting the sunlight. Towering above the roofs and the haze was a tall mill chimney. It all looked far away.

Dudley sat down at the roadside, suddenly exhausted. Grip flopped a few feet away from him, jaws agape, his eyes narrow and black above them fixed on his master's face. The boy was startled to see him there for, as he ran away from the dark pond, so in his heart had he run away from Grip and he hadn't known the dog had followed him.

'Go away. Leave me alone,' he cried at him, jumping up and making threatening movements with his arms and legs.

Grip ran off a little way, halted, then ran a bit further as Dudley came after him again. Normally he wouldn't have run, even though Dudley meant to hurt him, but he sensed the boy's mood, that he didn't want him anywhere near him.

'Aye, coward. Run. That's all tha's good for. Run!' Dudley yelled at him, picking up stones to throw at him and handfuls of gravel from the roadside.

Grip kept out of his reach, circling with dropped head and flattened tail, but not out of his sight. It was impossible to make him go away.

'Then stay here,' cried his master. 'Stay here and don't follow me ever again. I don't want to see thee any more. Stay here.'

Grip understood that command only too well. He lay down where he was, on the grass verge on the opposite side of the road, and watched Dudley's retreating figure, his good ear pricked, the other still dripping blood over his leg and neck. Once Dudley turned to look back at him and Grip sprang to all fours, ready for the command to follow.

'Stay there!' the boy yelled at him, his right arm lifted threateningly, and Grip sank down again, not understanding but obedient.

When the boy was out of sight he whined, but he waited for him as he had been taught, confident of his return.

Mill Cottages

Bill Kershaw asked no questions. A dog like Grip was best forgotten, certainly not to be mourned over, and he and his son went back to their usual round as if Grip had not been involved in their lives over the last year and more. Dudley refused to think about him at all. He put him altogether out of his mind because otherwise he could not bear his new loneliness and lack of purpose. Whenever he found his thoughts straying he quickly checked them. As far as he was concerned it was as if Grip were at the bottom of the pond, sunk for ever. There was no purpose in remembering.

He went to school every day without fail, even arriving early, and there wasn't a day when he didn't get into a fight with somebody, finding savage satisfaction in hitting out with his fists. He started the fights, always picking on lads bigger than himself and sometimes getting beaten, and every day he was called out after prayers at the morning assembly to be punished before the whole school. He only stopped fighting when there was no one left worth picking on.

He didn't go to the moor but sometimes, instead of going home after school, he would go to the recreation ground in the town park where he might find boys he could fight with. Or he would go along the canal bank to look for mischief or entertainment of some kind. There were usually a few children along there in the summer evenings, fishing for tiddlers which they stuck in jamjars. When they weren't looking he would throw the tiddlers back into the water, jamjar and all, or dare the boys to run across the locks after him or jump the half-open ones. Anything rather than go home too soon to find only his father and Madman in the kitchen.

Night-time was the worst, going up the stone staircase without the dog behind him, taking off his clothes without Grip to watch him, getting into bed and not feeling the springs sink as the dog jumped up after him, and no hard, warm head on which to rest his hand as sleep overtook him. It was difficult to fall asleep without that weight and warmth dragging the blankets off him and it was then when he found it hardest of all to keep memories out of his head and to stop himself from asking where Grip was now.

Could he still be on the moor, waiting for him, obeying his order to stay? Just as his stubbornness had made it difficult for him as a puppy to heed his master, so as he learned had that same stubbornness made him a slave of his commands. Thus he would have died in his efforts to bring him the badger, rather than give in, and so he knew he must stay until his master changed the command. If only his courage had equalled his stubbornness. Too little of one and too much of the other was in him. If only the spirit to fight had been there, Grip would have been unbeatable. Instead he was stubborn in his refusal to accept a challenge and was defeated by his own cowardice.

Reminding himself of this whenever his thoughts escaped him, Dudley hardened his heart. Although he had learned to feel love he had not yet discovered compassion.

A couple of weeks went by. The summer holidays were now near enough to be almost a reality. There was always plenty to do during those brief weeks of summer.

All the mills closed for a week at the same time and, except for the few who could afford boarding houses at Blackpool or Scarborough, The Crags became the holiday resort for the townspeople. Dudley and his father were kept busy from morning till night, supplying day trippers with food and drink, though Dudley did more washing up than anything else. The summer before he had resented this, with Grip's eyes expressing the longing that he himself felt for both of them to be away over the moors, but this year he was glad.

One morning the teacher made an announcement. She said that one of the girls in the class had found a dog on the moor and taken it home but that, as she couldn't keep it herself, she was looking either for its original owner or for someone who would like to give it a home.

'If you want to know anything else about it you must wait until break and ask May,' she said. 'We can't afford to waste time talking about it now. If you have any friends in other classes, you can let them know.'

Most of the class looked at May, glad of an excuse for chattering, but Dudley didn't turn round, although the words had pierced his heart. By then he had so much managed to put the dog out of his head that the news came as a shock, as if someone he had taken for dead was suddenly proved to be alive.

He spent the next two lessons wondering how Grip had come into her hands, for of course it was Grip she had found. If he had tired of 'staying', why hadn't he come home? Had he known that his master had rejected him? Had he been too much afraid to return? How long had he waited, an hour, a day, a week? Why had he gone with this girl?

When the bell rang for the end of lessons several boys and girls stopped to talk to May and were pushed out into the playground by the teacher still talking about the dog. Dudley had no intention of letting it be known that the dog was his, but he couldn't resist hovering on the edge of the group, needing an answer to his questions. He kept his back to the small gathering but when they saw that he was near they all moved away, afraid he was going to tease them. He only learned that May had two weeks to find a new home for the dog and that she lived at a place called Mill Cottages.

Dudley told himself it was only curiosity that made him decide to find out where Mill Cottages was. He wasn't going to let anyone know that Grip was his and he certainly wasn't going to go there. He would just follow May for a little way after school, without letting her realize it, and then go home.

He discovered she had a brother at the grammar school because first she went there to wait for him. It had to be her brother because they were so much alike with the same very fair hair and long, thin faces. Dudley felt an instinctive contempt for him. Everyone said the grammar-school boys were cissies because they wore uniforms and dressed up for cricket and football, and the headmaster's son went to the grammar school which was sufficient to condemn it out of hand.

Dudley followed them at a distance through half the streets of the town and stopped only when they turned into the alley which ran alongside Sutcliffe's woollen mill. He couldn't follow them any further without being seen so he waited for a while, pretending to be interested in the sweets in the little shop opposite the mill. The alley proved to be the back entrance to a row of cottages with black stone walls and black slate roofs, each one with a little backyard shut off from the alley by wooden doors, some well kept and brightly painted, others shabby or half broken. By the time Dudley had reached the cottages May and her brother had disappeared.

He stood there hesitating. Why did he want to know where they lived, anyway? What business was it of his? Better to go home and forget about it. However, something stronger than common sense urged him on and he strolled along the grass-tufted alleyway, mustering up a nonchalant air in case someone should see him, at the same time unable to prevent a faster beat to his heart at the knowledge that his dog was here somewhere, so near to him.

Suddenly he heard Grip bark. There was no doubting that deep, strong tone, only a few yards away from him. Had Grip caught his scent, he wondered? Should he run?

The longing to see him was far too strong. Just one quick peep through the keyhole if there was one and then he'd be off. There was the door, its old red paint almost faded into the wood, but there were neither cracks nor keyholes. He could hear May talking.

'Good boy, Prince. There's a good lad. I know you're pleased to see me but you don't need to make so much noise. Aunty's giving lessons and she'll be so cross if you don't be quiet. Ssh!'

Grip went on barking and May exclaimed, 'What is it then? What's the matter?'

There was a momentary silence and, even as Dudley realized what was happening, he saw the latch lift and a second later was face to face with the grammar-school boy, May close behind him. He caught just a glimpse of Grip tied to a wall, lungeing towards him, before he dashed off down the lane, and he went on running long after he had lost the sound of Grip's frantic barks; running until they had gone from his head as well as his hearing, hating himself for his own weakness.

Prince

The next day Dudley didn't go to school. He went up to the moor and wandered about until eventually reaching the place where he had left Grip fifteen or twenty days ago. How long he now couldn't exactly remember. The sun was so hot that the tar on the road was melting and for some time he amused himself making patterns in it with a stone and pressing dents in it with his clogs. The sun shone on the town through a haze of smoke and Dudley saw the chimney of Sutcliffe's mill and wondered what Grip was doing right now in the backyard of one of those cottages in its shadow.

Prince she called him! What a daft name. A girl's name for a dog. What did she know about Grip? What right had she to give him away, or even to take him home in the first place? Why couldn't she have minded her own business? It was as his father said. No one in the town knew how to keep himself to himself. They were for ever interfering in other people's affairs.

He gave a contemptuous grunt as he dug his heel heavily into the tar again. She'd be making him soft with all her daft talk, or she'd be keeping him tied up, which he hated. He felt like going down there right then, marching up to the house and taking his dog away, but then . . .

He threw the tar-covered stone at the wall on the other side of the road.

How could Grip even go with her? What was he thinking of? Hadn't he told him to stay? Rage filled him. He should have drowned him. That's what he should have done. Grip was a no-good coward who'd gone off with the first person to click their fingers at him. A girl at that! He'd got no pride, that dog, no sense of shame. He was well rid of him. Let him be her pet if that's all he was good for. Who wanted a dog like that, anyway?

Then he remembered that May had said she could only keep him for two weeks. That just showed how daft she was. She probably hadn't seen as good a dog as that in all her life and she was going to get rid of him. That brother of hers wouldn't have any more sense either. He was glad they weren't going to keep Grip. They didn't deserve him.

Such were the conflicting thoughts and emotions that filled him that summer's day and he wished he could have found somebody to fight with, May's brother, for instance, anyone – he didn't care – but the moor was as lonely as he was and offered him neither challenge nor comfort.

When the headmaster came into the classroom with his cane the following morning Dudley was on his feet before being called. A deathly hush affected everyone as his obvious defiance brought the red-faced Mr Wilkes to inflict six of the heaviest strokes he could muster. Everyone hated and feared him and even the teacher was subdued when she got the class back to work. Dudley kept his head down and took no part in the lesson but she left him alone out of sympathy.

At break May came up to him in the playground. He was on his own by the railings, hands tucked under his arms, and he scowled at the sight of her. She was undeterred.

'Prince is your dog, isn't he?' she said. She talked more like the teacher than someone from Mill Cottages, which was as good a reason as any for Dudley to be suspicious of her.

'I don't know any dog called Prince,' he answered roughly, turning away.

She followed him.

'Well, you know who I mean. The dog I found. I call him Prince because . . . well, because he looks like a prince and I don't know his real name. What is it?' she added appealingly, trying to gain his attention.

'How should I know?'

He stared through the railings at the houses opposite, wishing she would go away, unable to meet her demanding grey eyes.

'He loves you, you know,' she went on. 'You don't know how much. You just left him on that road, didn't you, and he waited and waited for you but you didn't go back for him. Why didn't you?'

How could she know so much? Had she seen him? He was tempted to ask her, but that would mean letting her know she was right, getting involved again, and he didn't want that. He could sense that she cared for Grip but he wasn't going to be drawn into talking about him. He thought she would go away if he were silent, but she didn't. She climbed up on the railings beside him, making herself taller.

'Mr Wilkes really hurt you this morning, didn't he?' she said. She didn't seem to mind him not answering, quite capable of carrying on the conversation for both of them. 'Why do you keep getting yourself into trouble? I mean, you know what's going to happen if you play truant or if you're late. I hate Mr Wilkes. I think he's wicked. Don't you?' She swung up and down on the railings as she spoke. 'I'm scared of him. Aren't you?'

'He doesn't scare me,' Dudley conceded unwillingly, still not looking at her.

'But you must be scared of some things. I'm scared of lots of things. Really, I was scared of talking to you. I thought you'd be horrible. Nearly everybody's scared of you and if it hadn't been for Prince . . . My brother didn't want me to talk to you. He said Prince couldn't be your dog because – ' She stopped, suddenly realizing that she had better not tell Dudley what her brother had said. 'But he doesn't understand Prince like I do.'

She was silent for a minute and had stopped swinging on the railings when she asked, 'Why don't you want him?' Her persistence was wearing Dudley down. He wasn't used to having so many questions thrown at him and his instinct was to run away from her. But if he did that it would be admitting she was right. In a way, too, he wanted to talk to her, but he didn't know what to say. He chewed his bottom lip, dark eyebrows sullenly drawn, at war with himself.

'I wish he was my dog,' went on May. 'He's the most beautiful dog in the world. I wanted him to love me like he loves you, but he won't, you know. I think he likes me. He's always pleased to see me when I come home from school but, really, in his heart, he's still waiting for you.'

'Tha talks daft,' he said at last, gruffly.

'I've had him for four days now, at home I mean. Before that I used to take him food up to the moor. He wouldn't come with me, you see. He was waiting for you. At first he wouldn't even eat the food but in the end he just had to. He was beginning to like me a bit by then, too. Two weeks it was before he'd come with me. I think he knew then that you didn't care any more, because you don't care, do you?' Her voice was sharp with accusation and exasperation at his obduracy.

'Nay, I don't,' he yelled back at her, his dark eyes blazing with anger when at last he looked at her.

She shrank away as if he were going to hit her.

'He's thy dog now. Do what tha likes with him. It's nowt to do with me,' and he marched off, refusing to listen to her any longer.

After a moment she called after him. 'You are horrible,

just like everybody says. You're wicked and you don't deserve ever to have had a dog like Prince. I'm glad he's not yours and I'm not scared of you. I'm not even sorry for you any more.'

She blinked back tears as she spoke, tears he didn't see, tears of rage at his heartlessness and because, in spite of her words, she was scared of him. Her brother was right. He was a brute and she would never speak to him again.

May

In her own way May **was** as stubborn as both the dog and his master. Were it not so, the dog wouldn't be in her possession now, sleeping in the backyard because Jenny – the mongrel terrier bitch Aunty Eugie had rescued from a tinker who ill-treated her – went crazy with rage and excitement if he as much as poked his nose through the back door.

David had taken her to the moor that Sunday, looking for wild ponies. He was always looking for animals in his free time and spent hours watching birds and insects. His biggest ambition was to rear a baby badger and he had already built a home for one in the backyard. Aunty Eugie let him because the backyard was almost too small to be useful for anything and he already had mice, frogs and a rabbit out there. He had a notebook full of information he had collected on badgers, but although he spent hours in the woods, often in darkness, he never caught more than a glimpse of them.

That Sunday they didn't come across any wild ponies but they did find the dog sitting at the roadside, blood dripping from its mangled ear. There was something about him even then that made May understand he was waiting for someone, though she couldn't have said what it was. He wouldn't go with them; he really hardly looked at them. She had never seen a dog so aloof.

Such was the impression he made on her that she couldn't forget him. That night she had even dreamed about him, seeing him lonely and white against a darkening moorland sky, sitting, sitting, never moving from where he sat, his patient eyes filling her heart with such heaviness that she awoke to find tears on her cheeks and her throat choked with sorrow.

She had to see him again. She couldn't bear to dream of those patient eyes, to feel that sadness and awake with tears a second time. She had to make sure that whoever he had been waiting for had gone for him, and she didn't ask herself what she would do if the dog were still there. She didn't tell David because, although he was so good to her in many ways, he always laughed at her dreams and the next day, after school, she had gone up to the moor again to find the dog still waiting, just as she'd seen him before.

His ear was no longer bleeding but his faith was unchanged. He wasn't interested in her at all, although he did deign to look at her for a moment, and his patience exasperated her.

'Can't you see that you're wasting your time?' she had cried at him. 'Can't you see that no one is coming?'

She had always wanted to have a dog who would love her. Jenny didn't count. She only loved Aunty Eugie. Already she was wishing that this dog could be hers. Tentatively she had put her hand on his thick white skull. He had such gentle eyes that she couldn't feel afraid of him. Carefully she looked at him, aware of powerful muscles beneath the scarred and broken skin, longing to take care of him, to feel his love in exchange, but although she talked to him and touched him he didn't move his head or change his stance. She just didn't exist for him at all and he didn't care when she went away.

But she kept on going to see him, determined to win his

trust if not his love, unable to abandon him, until at last she knew he was pleased to see her, until at last he would accept food from her hands. She called him Prince and every day she went up to the moor with dread in her heart in case he wasn't there any more, in case someone had at last come for him, but there he always was and she began to hope that perhaps he was waiting for her now instead of that someone else.

Although she was anxious for him to go home with her, at the same time she was glad that he wouldn't. While he was on the moor he belonged entirely to her, or at least she could pretend that he did because the dog himself never in any way gave her to understand that he felt the same. He was never wildly excited when she arrived but his eyes would brighten and his tail would wag as soon as he saw her coming up the road.

He often gazed at her as if asking her something but sometimes the look was more anxious than questioning. Did he believe she would one day bring his true master along? Oh, how long would it be before he would surrender his other love and devote himself entirely to her? Even though Aunty Eugie had said she couldn't keep him and was growing impatient of her daily excursions to the moor, May was sure that once she saw him she would change her mind. Somehow she would make her. But first Prince would have to decide.

She never knew what made him go home with her after more than two weeks of resisting. He just went along as if it were the proper thing to do, as if he were not at last breaking with all he had clung to, as if he had made up his mind and that was that. Without any excitement he accepted the place in the yard, the rope round his neck, Jenny's jealousy of him, her aunt's and her brother's curiosity. And when he saw her he licked her fingers and face and wagged his tail.

She was beginning to hope that one day he would love her, when time had made him forget, but Aunty Eugie would give her no hope.

'We can't keep him in the house because of Jenny and when the cold weather comes he can't possibly stay in the yard. Besides, we can't afford to keep him. He eats such a lot.'

This was true. His appetite was four times Jenny's, not that he was given four times her food, but May knew he was always hungry and this worried her. His ear had healed by itself but he was visibly thinner than when she had first seen him and some of the lustre had gone from his coat.

May knew they were poor. She and her brother had lived with Aunty Eugie for most of their lives, ever since the death of their mother when May was only a few months old. Their father was an actor and at his wife's death he had gone off to America to try to make a name for himself in films, but the Depression had been too much for him and one day Aunty Eugie received a small parcel from a hospital there which contained his few belongings and a letter to say that he was dead. She herself was a widow whose husband had been killed in France during the war. He had married her, gone out there and died all within three weeks and all that she had was this cottage they had rented, a pension and a fading photograph. She gave piano lessons in the front room and also played for the local dancing school. She didn't really belong in this street of cramped cottages but it was all she could afford.

May had never worn a brand-new dress in her life and the best day of the week was Sunday, when they had cakes for tea, but it wasn't until she was told that she couldn't keep Prince that the real meaning of poverty came to her. It meant denying her the one thing she wanted, the one thing she loved.

Knowing that her days with Prince were numbered, she spent every available moment with him, sitting beside him in the backyard while she shucked peas or peeled potatoes, talking to him all the time, even sitting beside him to read, leaning against his strong flank, and not going in until it was time for bed because he couldn't go inside with her. David said she was silly, that she was making things harder for herself that way, but May didn't listen to him. He didn't love Prince as she did, so he didn't understand.

May was sure that in just a few more weeks Prince would love her as much as she loved him, if only Aunty Eugie would give her those weeks, but then Dudley Kershaw came up the alley that day after school, Prince heard and smelled him, and all his affection for her was forgotten. After that he was impatient of the backyard, heedless of her company. He had whined for a long time after the boy had gone and wouldn't eat his food, as if conscious of treachery in so doing. All the next day he was the same so May knew that Prince was Kershaw's dog even though he pretended to know nothing about him.

In the classroom she couldn't help but wonder about him in spite of his behaviour towards her. She sat a little way behind him across the aisle and, thinking of the dog she called Prince and the constancy with which he had bided so long on the moorland road, she had to ask herself what kind of boy he was, so dour, so brutish, so pitiless, yet commanding so much faith. There he sat, his hair as unkempt as the shirt with the worn collar under the green pullover laced with holes, oblivious of her curiosity, oblivious of her existence until now.

What did she know about him beyond what all the class knew – what everyone said because, really, no one knew anything about him at all? The teacher had given up trying to make him learn anything and he seemed to be in the classroom only as an example to the rest of what they might become if they didn't try hard enough. He had been in this class for two years already and was likely to stay there for ever, bigger and older than everyone else, a silent, uncaring outcast.

May had always secretly felt sorry for him. She was instinctively inclined towards all 'lame ducks', as her aunt called them, and made friends with the most unsuitable people. One birthday she had invited home to tea the only girl who never got invitations from anybody. She hardly knew her name but saw her always alone in the playground if not surrounded by a teasing, hostile crowd. So she took the poor girl home, even though her best friend had threatened not to speak to her for a week, happily anticipating her pleasure. But she was turned away at the door by a horrified Aunty Eugie and May was severely lectured and never allowed to take anyone home to tea again. It was then that she learned that the girl had lice, that her brothers were suffering with ringworm, and for a long time afterwards Aunty Eugie inspected her very closely, expecting her to develop all sorts of dreadful diseases. But May only felt even more sorry for the girl and wished that Aunty Eugie hadn't been so cruel to her, especially when she was usually sympathetic to people in need.

She was always too afraid of Dudley ever to want to make friends with him but she often wished that he wouldn't be late for school or play truant so frequently because she dreaded seeing him punished, even though he didn't seem to care. Didn't he care, or was it only pretence? Was he only pretending not to care about the dog, too? Was he really such a ruffian and a bad lot as everyone said? For the dog to love him so much she knew there had to be some good in him somewhere, and she had two weeks in which to find it if she wanted to save Prince's life.

85

Dudley talks

The summer holidays came and with the breaking up of school there was no chance for May to see Dudley again unless she was prepared to brave him at The Crags. She would never have done this, for she was not the most courageous of people, had not her love for the dog outweighed her fear of his master.

She had thought that Prince had begun to accept her, to care for her, because so it had seemed, but since Dudley had made his appearance in the alley she knew that he only impatiently tolerated her. Once again he almost ignored her existence and hardly even ate the food she put down for him. He would lie the whole day, head on paws, the light gone from his dark eyes whose gaze never left the shabby yard door, and all of May's warmth meant nothing to him.

May had told Aunty Eugie about Dudley. They could only guess at his reasons for abandoning the dog but, as the days went by and he showed no interest in recovering him, they had to assume that he didn't care any more. May begged to be allowed to keep him and it wasn't hard-heartedness on her aunt's part that made her say no. Jenny already lived on the very few left-overs they had and, in order to be able to buy her the cheap butcher's scraps that made up her main diet, she had had to find another pupil to pay for them. It wasn't easy to find pupils. Not many parents could afford piano lessons for their children.

She regretted having allowed May to bring the dog home. May loved him and nothing she could say or do would change her feelings. But she couldn't get rid of Jenny to give a home to this second dog and she couldn't afford to feed them both.

'But he's not even hungry,' May had cried to her. 'He really eats very little.'

'He doesn't eat enough. Look how thin he is. He's pining away for that boy you say he belongs to.'

The two weeks Aunty Eugie had given May to find Prince a new home had passed but, because of May's determination, she agreed to give her a little more time, not without some heartsearching, sure that it would be harder in the end for May to part with him. She could see more clearly than the girl that the dog's health was deteriorating from day to day. The hot weather made him thirsty and he drank a lot of water. It was this that mainly kept him alive because the scraps on his dish shrivelled in the sun or were snapped up by Jenny who came out into the yard to steal them, and growl at him, whenever she could.

At last she put into words the possibility that May had not wanted to accept. 'If he doesn't get back to his master I think he'll die. He just doesn't want to live without him.'

'I'll make him love me, Aunty. I know I will.'

'You can't, May. He might come to accept you of his own accord again, but you can't make him love you. If he hadn't seen that boy again . . .' Gently she added, 'Really, I think we'd be doing him a kindness if we had him put to sleep. He's so unhappy. You can see he is.'

May couldn't accept this reasoning. She couldn't accept that anything would rather die than live. If she couldn't make Prince love her then she would have to make his master take him back. But to go to The Crags on her own was far too daunting and she asked David to go with her.

May couldn't imagine life without David. He made toys for her out of wood and paper, he often took the responsibility for things she did wrong as well as the punishment for them, he took her on nearly all his expeditions in spite of his usual threats never to take her again, and tried to teach her to be brave and strong so that his friends couldn't call her a cissy. He made her climb walls and trees, hold caterpillars, spiders and even worse creatures, and he sometimes let her look after his animals for him. But he was also demanding and hard to please and he wouldn't have taken her to The Crags had not Aunty Eugie persuaded him. He didn't approve of her interest in Dudley and certainly couldn't accept that there might be some good in him.

He was slightly older than Dudley and knew something of him although they went to different schools. He was scornful of May's excuses for his behaviour and thought he probably deserved all the punishments he got. He didn't really approve of Aunty Eugie giving way to May's pleadings, either, but in the end he said he would go with her though he didn't think it would do any good.

May wanted to take Prince with them but he wouldn't forsake his vigil in the yard. In vain she pulled at the lead she had slipped round his neck, telling him she was going to take him home, but he didn't understand her and refused to budge. They found Dudley sitting on the wall opposite the inn, trying to chip bits off it with a stone. His expression of sullen boredom became one of suspicion when he saw them approach. May and David stopped a few feet away and, when the silence became too embarrassing, May broke it, saying, 'We've come about the dog.'

'What dog?' Dudley's expression didn't change but there was a threat in his voice.

88

'You know what dog,' answered David crossly. 'The one we're looking after for you.'

Both he and May could sense Dudley's antagonism towards him. May took hold of his arm, her face anxious. She had seen Dudley start so many fights and was frightened for her brother.

'He's sick,' she cried. 'Pining away. He wants to be with you. Please take him back.'

'I told thee before. It's nowt to do with me,' and he went on striking one stone against another, trying to make sparks.

'You're a coward,' David accused him, growing red-faced with emotion. 'You don't want to face your responsibilities. He's your dog. If you don't want him you should do something about it, not leave it to someone else. Only cowards behave like that.'

Dudley slipped off the wall and stalked up to David, his face dark with resentment.

'Take that back or I'll knock thee down,' he threatened.

'I won't,' said David, 'and I'm not fighting you either. You think that knocking me down is going to change things. Well it isn't. You'll still be a coward and – '

The next second Dudley's right arm had flashed out and David was sitting on the ground, blood gushing from his nose. May turned to him with a cry of dismay but he pushed her aside as he got up, holding his nose, his eyes watering with pain.

'It's all you know, isn't it?' he said scornfully, his voice shaky in spite of the dignity May knew he was trying to muster. 'You think you've solved everything now. All right, perhaps we won't come again, but that doesn't change the fact that you abandoned your dog in the most cowardly way and haven't even got the guts to admit it's yours. Come on, May. Let's go home.'

He turned away. For a moment May hesitated, struck

by the expression on Dudley's face. Despair and bewilderment were mirrored in his eyes. She was tempted to go up to him but she couldn't find the right words. In the end, she ran along the dusty road after David, aching in her heart for both of them.

A few days later she was sitting on the canal bank with David, trying not to say anything because he said she drove the fish away with her chatter, feeling sorry for the worms he had dug up and wishing they didn't have to be put on his hook. She felt sorry for the fish, too, but didn't dare say so to her brother. She was wishing Prince was with her, wishing even that she hadn't left him alone, eternally waiting, and then she saw Dudley coming towards them, diffident of expression.

He stopped a little way off and watched them, looking as unkempt as usual in a collarless shirt that was too big for him and his trousers frayed at the bottoms. David ignored him and May tried to do the same for a while, but the way he kept staring at them made her feel certain that he wanted to say something, if only she would give him the chance.

She got up and went over to him.

'How's Grip?' he asked, barely meeting her eyes.

'Grip! Is that his name?'

He nodded.

'I like that,' she said enthusiastically. 'It's better than Prince. Prince doesn't really suit him, does it?'

'How is he?' asked Dudley again, curtly.

May could never know how much it had cost him to approach her, how much he had struggled against this softness towards his dog which both weakened and shamed him.

'I wish you'd come and see him,' she said earnestly. 'He misses you so much. My aunt says he'll die if you don't come for him.'

'Stupid,' said Dudley roughly. 'That's all he is.'

'No he's not,' defended May hotly. 'He loves you.'

'Love is for cissies, for girls, for cowards like him.'

'You don't know anything about love or cowardice. Love is what your dog is doing, waiting for you, never giving up hope. A coward wouldn't wait like he does, two weeks on his own on the moors and now in our backyard.'

He hardly eats. He doesn't care about anything but you.'

'It's just daft talk,' insisted Dudley roughly, turning away from her to look across the fields that bordered that side of the canal.

'Then why have you come?'

He didn't answer. May glanced at David but his back was towards both of them. She knew he would have nothing more to do with Dudley, not because he was scared of him but because he despised him.

'Tell me about him,' she urged after a long silence. 'How did he come to be yours?'

Dudley found himself talking. He still stared over the fields, screwing up his eyes against the sun, or perhaps at painful memories. At first his sentences were short and reserved. They came slowly because he had to find the right words to be able to tell this girl about Grip. He had never talked much to anyone before but gradually the story was dragged out of his memory, out of his heart.

Listening to him, May realized that her love for the dog was nothing compared to his, even though his had been given with hardness and intransigence. Now she could understand the dog's devotion, too. They belonged to each other.

She couldn't understand Dudley's hopes and ambitions for Grip any more than she could make him understand that his way of thinking was barbaric, cruel. To Dudley, being cruel meant making a dog fight when it wasn't fit or neglecting it when a contest was over. He knew some men were cruel with their dogs, but it was the men who were bad, not the sport. It took a lot of time, effort and money to develop a first-class fighting dog, which was why bad dogs couldn't be kept and good dogs were usually well cared for.

'So Grip is a bad dog,' said May at last. 'He won't fight, so he's no good?'

Dudley nodded.

'Do you really think he's a coward?' she asked. 'Do you think my brother was a coward the other day because he wouldn't fight you? Because he's not, you know. He'd fight you or anyone if he had to, if it was for a good reason, but not just for the sake of fighting. Perhaps Grip is the same.'

Dudley didn't answer. David's accusation had hurt him, perhaps because he knew there was some truth in it. He hadn't had the courage to drown Grip as he'd promised, he hadn't had the courage to admit his ownership, he hadn't had the courage to wipe him out of his life. What was all this if not cowardice? He was very much confused.

'If he'd fight but one fight,' he cried out at last. 'Happen that'd be enough.'

'Perhaps he will one day, when he has to.'

She could see by his expression that he doubted it.

'Won't you just come and see him?' she begged. 'We could go now, while David's still here.'

He shook his head.

'Up on the moor then. I'll make him come up to the moor with me tomorrow. Will you be there? Where you left him? Where I found him?'

She thought he was going to refuse but at last he nodded briefly, as if afraid to commit himself with words, and then he ran off. May went back to David, wondering if she had achieved anything at all.

Warmth and resentment

It rained heavily the next morning but Dudley went anyway. There would be nobody wanting tea or ginger beer at The Crags that day so his father wouldn't miss him if he wasn't around. The moors were bleak on a wet day, the ground hardly distinguishable from the sky and whole areas lost in greyness, but Dudley noticed neither their aspect nor the rain, aware only of the keen pain in his heart. Excitement? Dread? He didn't know what it was, but it went from his heart to his stomach and even shivered through his limbs. He was glad to be running and climbing, panting hard.

May was waiting for him on the road, a forlorn-looking figure in a dark green raincoat that was too small for her. Grip wasn't with her.

'He wouldn't come,' she explained, her pale face wet with rain. 'He thinks you're going back to the yard one day and he's waiting for you there.'

Dudley hunched his shoulders and began kicking the roadside turf. He knew what she was going to say next and didn't know how he would, or should, answer her.

'Come back home with me. Come and see him. He's waited so long. . . .'

He went on kicking the grass, more savagely now. How could he bear to see Grip again and not take him home? He couldn't. He couldn't, and yet . . .

The words came harshly at last. 'All right. But only five minutes. I won't stay. I can't.'

May's delight showed in her eyes, on her lips, as she cried, 'Come on then. Race you down the hill.'

She pelted off, arms stretched out, pretending she was a sailing ship battling against wind and rough seas, zooming, zigzagging across the road. For a moment Dudley just stood watching her, still hesitating, not knowing what to make of her. She was halfway down the hill before he overtook her, for once not caring about anything. He waited for her at the bottom of the hill and they walked the rest of the way, May chattering tirelessly, telling him about David and his mania for collecting animals and how she'd helped him build the badger den, as well as everything she could think of about Grip. Dudley marvelled that anyone could talk so much without getting breathless. He hardly said anything himself. He didn't need to.

At last they came to the alley and May's backyard, hair dripping, faces wet. Grip began barking. Could he smell Dudley or did he recognize his footsteps? Whatever it was, he knew, and his barks were deep, wild and demanding.

Then Dudley saw him, straining at the end of his rope, tail waving madly, black eyes gleaming, and the barks became yelps, cries, whimpers all mixed together as he went on his knees beside him and crushed him into his arms. How good it was to feel him again, the eager tongue slobbering over him, the paws clawing at him, hurting him in their eagerness. He could hardly bear the choked sounds that Grip uttered and clung to him with his face pressed against a strong, wet shoulder, unable to speak.

It was a while before Grip grew reasonably calm. He kept dancing about, his hard tail whacking both May's and Dudley's legs, and neither noticed the rain or how wet they were getting until Aunty Eugie came out, drawn by Jenny's frantic barks from inside the house, and exclaimed at their state. She couldn't persuade Dudley to go inside but seeing his dark eyes shining with joy, his hands constantly fondling the ears of the dog pressed restlessly against him, she didn't insist. She went away but came back later with two thick hunks of bread and dripping.

'It'll get wet if you don't eat it quickly,' she warned with a smile, but it disappeared fast, most of it down Grip's hungry throat.

'Come back again,' May begged Dudley when at last he said he must go. 'We'll take Grip out for walks together. We can do that, can't we?'

Dudley nodded and this time when he ran off down the alley, Grip's barks sounded joyfully in his heart and he couldn't have stopped grinning even if he had wanted to. As he neared home, however, his pleasure faded. He began to have doubts of the promise May had dragged out of him, to go back there, to take Grip for walks with her. The whole idea was so contrary to his solitary nature that once the first enthusiasm was gone it was hard to imagine himself even talking to May again, let alone sharing her company. But there was Grip. The dog's hold over his heart was stronger than any doubt in his mind, and the next day he was at the back gate again, knocking uncertainly, more unsure of himself than of the welcome awaiting him.

Grip went frantic with delight again and with hardly a word to May beyond a gruff acknowledgement of her presence, Dudley untied his dog and went off with him. There were no thoughts in his head just then, only feelings in his heart, and May didn't care how rude he seemed because she could understand what he was feeling.

He made straight for the moor, Grip dancing along beside him, black eyes aglow, jaws stretched into a grin, and May hurried in their wake, inviting herself along, not caring where they were going as long as she could be with them, sharing their joy. Every now and then Grip jumped up to paw at Dudley, as if unable to contain his joy, and Dudley patted him fiercely then went hurrying on. May patted Grip too and called out to him and he gave her a glance and a lick before returning his attention to his master.

Up on the moor they romped and fought and chased each other as they had always done, the tugging, buffeting wind part of their game, and when Dudley could play no longer and threw himself back on the turf, shading his eyes from the sun, Grip went to lie down beside him, thrusting his heavy muzzle across the boy's chest, heaving a sigh of contentment. He didn't close his eyes, keen to capture the boy's every mood, and his tail beat an untiring tattoo on the grass.

Although almost entirely ignored by them May didn't feel an outsider, so much pleasure did she find in just watching them. She was used to being ignored by David on some of his expeditions and was happy just to be there. She threw herself down beside Dudley when the game was over, stroking Grip, and no longer wished he could be her dog, knowing this could never be. She was glad just to be able to have a share in him.

On the way back home she began to talk and now Dudley was more prepared to listen, his mood softened by sheer contentment. He didn't say much himself but that was never any problem for May. She could rattle on for hours, much to David's annoyance, and, with no one to stop her, talked until they were back at Mill Cottages once more.

Finding she made no demands upon him, Dudley

found it easier and easier to accept May's companionship. They didn't always go to the moor. Sometimes they went to the fields not far beyond the mill through which ran a stream where they paddled and made dams for Grip to splash in. Sometimes they got no further than May's backyard where May's voice was accompanied by the unending clatter of the mill machinery. When it was hot the mill doors and windows were open and all up and down the alley the noise hammered and clamoured until nobody really heard it at all.

May showed Dudley her books and games, things that puzzled and surprised him because there was nothing of this kind in his own home. He thought books had only to do with school and although some games, such as dominoes and checkers, fascinated him for a few hours, he was usually hankering to be on the moor with his dog where he could always feel alone even though May never abandoned him.

It was hard for him to understand the ways that May and her family took for granted. Just the fact that they expected him to love his dog, and talked of it with such naturalness, had him confused. Love was for women and people in books. It had nothing to do with real life, with men or with dogs. Love was a form of treachery which left a man without sense or will-power, made him a coward, made him lose himself. This was all Dudley knew of love, taught to him by his father over the years with words as brief as they were scornful. Had his father ever accused him of loving Grip he would have denied it hotly, feeling all the shame of it, and yet these people not only accepted and encouraged it but went out of their way to show warmth towards him, all except David.

He didn't approve of the way May played and talked and spent her time with Dudley and he went off alone to look for badger sets or rabbit holes, a notebook tucked in his pocket and something to eat in a paper bag. He would have nothing to do with either the dog or the boy and kept out of their way.

Grip's appetite came back and now even May could see that Aunty Eugie would never be able to afford to feed him as required. The little plateful of scraps put down for him disappeared in a flash. He would look up anxiously for more, licking his big jaws, eyes expressing his want, and then go round and round the plate with his tongue as if to get more sustenance out of it somehow.

Aunty Eugie began to grow impatient. She was prepared to let May try to persuade Dudley to take the dog back. She allowed her to be in his company in spite of her original doubts, but she couldn't go on feeding someone else's dog – and one with such a big appetite – indefinitely. She talked of going to see Dudley's father or the police and May tried desperately to make her understand that neither of these actions would help Grip, that both would cause his destruction.

'Then he's got to be found another home,' she insisted sternly. 'I just can't keep him much longer, May, and I intend to tell that boy so myself. I feel sorry for him, I feel sorry for them both, but I can't afford it, May. I'm sorry.'

David resented all this interest in Dudley and the problems the dog was causing. Unlike his sister, he was keenly aware of their aunt's struggle to survive from week to week. May, with her head lost in stories and dreams, never noticed how tired she was at the end of the day, never wondered how she managed to pay for the next pair of shoes from the second-hand shop round the corner. May's heart was easily touched by stray dogs and suffering mermaids but she was as thoughtless as a sparrow. Dudley seemed to have taken over the backyard, taken over his sister, letting them keep his dog for him but offering nothing in return.

He knew Aunty Eugie didn't really want to talk to him. She was too good to want to make anyone suffer and so he took it upon himself to tell Dudley what he thought. The memory of that punch on the nose still rankled and he wanted to hurt him if he could. It was no more than he deserved. Knowing what Dudley was like, he realized that he might have to fight him, but this time he was prepared to, determined to make Dudley understand that he wasn't wanted at Mill Cottages.

Neither Aunty Eugie nor May knew of his plan and it wasn't until halfway through the next morning, after May had waited in vain for Dudley to turn up as he'd promised and only David eventually appeared, with a swollen, discoloured eye, a split lip and blood on his shirt, that they learned what had happened. With his usual honesty, David admitted that he had started the fight and come off worst in it, but he didn't care. He was certain Dudley wouldn't bother them again.

May burst into tears but whether she cried for her brother or for Dudley, or for both, not even she could tell. Perhaps really she was crying for Grip.

A popular breed

Days went by and Dudley felt his loneliness more keenly than ever before. It had been bad enough without Grip but now that he felt himself rejected by May and her family he hardly knew what to do with himself. At first rage against David had kept him from caring. Those people meant nothing to him, after all. If he'd had any sense at all he would have remembered what his father always told him – to keep away from the townspeople, to keep himself to himself. Like that no one could cause him any trouble. No one could hurt him.

Against his wishes, he kept remembering May and the comfort of her backyard, playing games with her, listening to her stories, Grip between them, dripping saliva on their bare legs as he panted in the summer's heat. He didn't know why he missed going there. He only knew that he did and the days were longer than they had ever been before.

He knew how much May felt for her brother and began to wish he hadn't accepted his challenge. She would never forgive him, never talk to him again probably. Not only would he lose Grip. He would also lose the first friendship of his life.

Angrily he told himself that May didn't matter. He only wanted Grip back and then he would forget all about her. He would find a time when everyone was away from the house then go to the yard and take Grip away. He would bring him back home and somehow make his father accept him. There must be a way of teaching him to fight, of redeeming the character he had lost.

The very thought of approaching his father filled him with fear. Although nothing had been said he knew his father believed he had drowned Grip weeks ago. How to tell him now that he hadn't; that he hadn't had the courage to go through with it? This confession alone would be sufficient for him to deny his request to have the dog back. Besides, it would call up all his father's contempt.

He didn't know what to do. Although there was hardly another thought in his head, he couldn't find the courage to speak to his father. He remembered how David had called him a coward and, although he struggled against admitting it, in the end he knew it was true. He had run away from many things. It was time to face up to them.

One evening, when the day's business was over and the two were alone in the kitchen, Madman in his usual place on the rug in front of the fire, which even in summertime was necessary in this cold house, Dudley, hardly breathing, made his confession.

'Dad . . . I didn't drown Grip after all.'

Bill Kershaw was in his armchair, facing the fire, the dog not far from his feet. He didn't look at his son as he answered, 'Aye, I know.'

'Tha knows?'

'I knew tha hadn't the guts to do it but I didn't give much thought on it at the time. Tha looked sick enough about it, anyway. Like a dead duck. A few days later I happened by the pond and found the rope there. I knew then tha hadn't done it but I didn't say nowt. What for?'

Although it hurt him to stand so low in his father's estimation, Dudley had to go on.

'I want him back, Dad.'

Bill Kershaw didn't answer.

'I said I want him back.'

'He's thy dog. Do as tha likes with him.'

'I can have him back?' His surprise was cautious.

'If thee wants him, thee must keep him. I'll not spend

another penny on him nor be responsible for him in this house.'

'He'd be champion for breeding. He's a bonnie-looking dog. Tha's said thaself he's got looks.'

'Aye, but with his reputation who does tha think will want him to sire their pups? Tha's got to breed for character more than looks.'

'Not if tha doesn't want dogs for fighting. Nay, there's people now that breed dogs for looks.'

Bill Kershaw made a scornful noise. 'I'll not have any of Madman's blood going to make weaklings. Tha's forgotten I had a stake in that dog, too. If he were mine I'd drown him. Bad blood's best got rid of.'

'Tha won't let me use him as a stud dog then if I bring him back?' went on Dudley, relentlessly. He couldn't give up the fight yet.

'I've already said. He's thy dog. It's nowt to do with me.'

'But – '

'Happen there's nowt more to be said,' interrupted his father with a challenging stare, and Dudley understood what he meant.

He wouldn't stop him bringing Grip back but, if he did, he would consider him fair game for Madman's teeth. There would be no more careful vigilance to keep them apart. The first time Grip got in Madman's way would be his last. How could he tell if, while he was at school, his father might not deliberately set the dog on Grip? It had been hard enough in the past to keep the jealous Madman at bay. Only his implicit obedience to his master's wishes had saved Grip before. Now there would be no voice to tell him no.

That night Dudley lay in bed too desperate to sleep. It seemed he had lost everything, even the hope that May had managed to keep alive. The idea of using Grip for breeding had been hers. It hadn't occurred to him.

Her aunt had a medical encyclopaedia in two volumes, at least twenty years old but full of fascinating information. As well as describing most human ailments and their cures, it also covered all kinds of domestic animals, plants and trees. There were photographs of the many different breeds of dogs, horses, cows and pigs with diagrams showing useful things such as how to give a cat pills or to keep a dog from removing bandages. One day she had brought these volumes out to the yard and they had gone through them, stopping for a long time at the section on dogs.

Dudley still remembered that it was entitled 'Man's Faithful Friend – How to Treat Him in Health and Sickness', because May had exclaimed, 'What a lovely way of writing about dogs! I always thought encyclopaedias were stuffy books.'

There were five pages of photos. Until then Dudley had never known there were so many different kinds of dogs in the world. He thought he knew just about every breed of ratter and terrier but there were dogs on those pages he would never ever see in a lifetime. At the top of the third page, between a Scottie and a Skye Terrier, was a photo of a dog which looked almost exactly like Grip, a bit thinner perhaps but with the same stance and expression.

'What does it say?' he had asked May with excitement. The book was on her lap.

'A popular breed, resulting from a cross between a bulldog and an English terrier,' she read.

'Is that all?' Impatiently he had dragged the book towards him. 'It doesn't say much, does it? Happen I could've written more than that.'

'It doesn't say much about any of them,' May tried to placate him. 'But it means that Grip is a pure-bred dog, worth a lot of money. He wouldn't be in this book if he wasn't. You could use him for breeding. You could make a lot of money out of him. I know about that because our doctor's got two Scotch collies and he makes lots of money out of them, everybody says.'

'My dad uses Madman for breeding sometimes,' Dudley had told her, remembering. 'He gets money like that, too,' and they had sat for a long time, talking of Grip's possibilities, sure they had found a purpose for him at last.

If it hadn't been for May . . . And now because of what he had done to her brother he couldn't even see her again, her or Grip, unless he could find some way to show that he hadn't really meant it. If he hadn't been so hasty with his fists . . . The triumph he had felt at flattening David had turned to bitterness. For the first time in his life he regretted his victory in battle.

Peace offering

The next night Bill Kershaw and two acquaintances plundered a badger's set in the woods at The Crags. They went with spades and a couple of excited terriers to dig them out, Madman accompanying his master as usual, and well after midnight returned with a full-sized adult and three cubs in their sacks. Dudley was awakened by the noise of the dogs and the men's heavy boots on the stone floors, but it wasn't until the next morning that he discovered what had been brought back, when his father told him to go and dig up as many worms as he could find in case they were hungry.

'What's tha going to do with them all?' he asked when he returned with a jamjar full of worms, as well as a few black beetles.

'I don't know yet. Hadn't expected to find so many. If we can keep the young'uns alive they'll do for baiting this winter.'

Dudley went down to the cellar and looked at the four animals in the box which had last held a badger on Grip's one night of glory. The cubs were pressed close against their mother who uttered a gruff bark of fear, or warning, when the shadow of the boy fell over her. He was surprised to see how big they were. The cubs must have weighed ten pounds or more. The food he had brought would hardly be enough for a single one of them, assuming they could be tempted to eat in captivity.

He shook the worms out on to the tin lid his father had provided and pushed it into the box, but the terrified badgers only crushed closer together and ignored the offering. Very soon the large black beetles had crawled away. The worms were more slothful.

Watching them, Dudley recalled May telling him how much her brother had wanted to find and rear a badger cub. Wouldn't he like to be here now, seeing these three! Perhaps if he took David a badger, May would forgive him and be friends with him again.

Dudley made a deal with his father. He would look after the badgers, dig for worms and other creatures all day long if necessary, if he could have one of the badgers for himself, the weakest one – it wouldn't matter which – as long as he could do what he liked with it.

'What's up then? What does tha want it for?'

'I promised one to a boy at school, that's all.'

Bill Kershaw thought for a while. There was no doubt the cubs would need a lot of feeding. They would need berries and fruit as well as worms and beetles and perhaps a dead rabbit or two. The chances were they wouldn't survive until winter but, in the meantime, the feeding of them would be hard work.

'Fair enough,' he said at last. 'But tha'd better keep at it. They'll be needing buckets full of worms before they've finished, as well as cleaning out and all the rest of it. I'll sort one out for thee.'

He gave him a female, the smallest of the three, and it yelped and whickered in the sack most of the way to Mill Cottages, sounding very much like a frightened puppy. May was in the yard and both Grip's excitement and May's surprise were shortened by their curiosity about the creature in the sack, which began struggling as soon as it felt solid ground beneath it. Grip began pushing the sack with his nose, making the cub yelp louder than ever.

'It's a badger,' explained Dudley. 'I'll let it out if tha's careful not to get bit. Keep Grip out of the road.'

He tipped the cub out of the sack and the first thing it did was rush to the den David had built, dashing between Grip's legs, instinctively seeking the darkness. All May saw was a flash of grey and white. Grip was about to dive through the door after it but Dudley grabbed hold of the rope round his neck and held him back.

'She'll not be out of there in a hurry,' he said. 'Tha'd best wait till thy brother's here. Happen tha'll get thy fingers bit if tha puts a hand in there.'

'Poor little thing,' cried May. 'It must be terrified.'

May tried peering in through the low door but it was too dark to see anything. She could hear snufflings of panic. It was almost as if she could feel its heart-beats.

'Best leave it be for a bit,' advised Dudley. He knew what a badger's teeth could do and even though this was only a cub he had a respect for it.

'Oh, if only David hadn't gone off this morning! He'll be so thrilled,' cried May.

Dudley grinned. All he wanted was the right to be back in this yard, Grip licking his face, May pleased with him. He'd dig up whole cartloads of worms for that.

The badger healed the breach between the two boys. They didn't become friends and they never had much to say to each other, unless it had to do with the badger which May christened Becky, but David was grateful and therefore polite. Even Aunty Eugie was mollified for a time, affected by David's contentment. They all spent a lot of time watching Becky, talking to her, trying to make her understand that they meant her no harm, and Grip would sometimes let out frustrated yelps, tired of being forgotten.

Dudley made Grip understand that he mustn't harm the badger who, encouraged by titbits and saucers of milk, was young enough to quickly abandon her instinctive fear of dogs and humans. David was the only one who handled her and he seemed to sense just how to approach her. Earlier he had laughed at his sister's dedication to Grip but already he was equally affected by this woodland animal and spent hours just watching her or nursing her on his knees while she slept in the sunlight.

The badgers at the inn didn't fare so well. The female would eat nothing she was offered and before she became sickly and useless Bill Kershaw used her at a baiting so that only the two cubs were left. They received none of the attention that Becky was getting, partly because Dudley didn't have the time for it and also because he knew his father would be furious if he turned them into docile pets. He got up very early each morning to collect as many snails and worms as he could, knowing like the birds that this was the best time of day to find them, and he gave them bread and milk as he had seen David do, but they remained lustreless and disinterested, lacking the will to survive.

Bill Kershaw transferred them to the outhouse after carefully examining it for possible escape routes and here they were happier, burrowing among the ferns and bracken which Dudley brought in armloads from the wood, but he never saw them play as Becky did and they were always frightened of him. They spent most of their time sleeping but when he threw them a few dead mice or green acorns before going to bed he could hear them shuffling about.

His renewed friendship with May, the time he spent with her laughing over the antics of Becky and Grip who had quickly reached an understanding, as well as the hours he spent hunting for badger food and helping his father with summer visitors, kept Dudley so busy that his urgent longing to have Grip home with him was somewhat abated. He saw the dog nearly every day, he went to bed exhausted and satisfied, and he had successfully pushed from both heart and mind the problems that had harried him for so long. Except for when Grip was a puppy and they had been free to roam together over the moors with dreams not yet tarnished and hopes not shattered, he was happy as he had never been before.

Banishment

David, May and Aunty Eugie discovered that a badger in the backyard had its inconveniences, especially when it shared its home with a dog. Becky spent most of the daylight hours sleeping, although she could always be coaxed out of her den at the rattle of a spoon against a plate and would play quite happily once awake. At night-time she was wide awake and eager to play, with all the vigorous energy she had stored up during the day. They were to learn that there was nothing more boisterous than a badger cub with a playmate, and Becky had Grip to play with.

Although Grip was tied up there was enough rope to give him sufficient movement for Becky's requirements. All she wanted to do was wrestle, chase or be chased, and Grip was only too willing to satisfy her. Although he weighed a good thirty pounds more than she did and could easily have killed her, in his games with Becky, which were sometimes extremely rough, he was the master of control and gentleness.

She would charge at his legs, trying to bowl him over, using her head and body as a battering ram, and he would grab her by the scruff of her neck, growling and threatening, but never doing more than wetting her hair. She would nip his tail and legs, taking good care to protect her nose which was the one sensitive part of her. If Grip accidentally banged or scratched it in their tussles, she would yelp and run off to the darkness of her den, but soon she would be back again, asking for more.

These mock battles often took place after midnight and it wasn't long before the neighbours began to complain. She was a hefty little animal and one night in her games with Grip the whole badger den, so carefully constructed by David with bits of wood collected from here and there, collapsed with a clatter which set most of the dogs in the street in alarm.

'If it weren't for Grip, Becky would probably sleep all night,' David insisted.

'That's not fair,' cried May. 'Grip never used to make a sound at night till Becky came along. It's she that wakes him up. She always starts it.'

'I don't care which one starts it,' said their aunt sternly, harassed by their angry neighbours. 'The fact is, we've got half the street up in arms and the backyard isn't really big enough for either of them. David, I'm afraid you're going to have to take Becky back to the woods and, May, when Dudley comes I'm going to have to tell him he must either do something about Grip himself or expect to lose him. Things can't go on like this any longer.'

Both May and David were equally subdued. David started gathering up the bits of wood he had so carefully put together, piling them up against the wall. It wasn't worthwhile reconstructing the den if Becky wasn't to be allowed to stay. May watched him, sitting beside Grip, crushed with unhappiness. This time she knew Aunty Eugie meant what she said. She was thoroughly fed up with both animals. Becky was curled up in a corner, fast asleep, unaware of the havoc she had caused.

'I can't just take her back to the woods and let her go free,' said David despairingly. 'She doesn't know how to fend for herself. She won't know how to find her own food or anything. She hasn't got a home any more.'

'We haven't had her all that long. Perhaps she hasn't forgotten yet. It's worse for Grip. At least Becky's going to be free. If Dudley won't take Grip he'll be put to sleep.'

'Well, you've known that all along. Aunty never told me before that I couldn't keep a badger. She let me build this den and everything.'

'Because she didn't know what having a badger was going to be like. None of us knew. We didn't know she was going to be so smelly either.'

'She's not smelly all the time,' defended David. 'It's only when she gets excited.'

'And she's excited all the time, playing with Grip. She even makes him smell.'

'It's Kershaw's fault we've got Grip.'

'And who brought the badger? If it wasn't for him you wouldn't have had Becky, would you?'

They stopped quarrelling when Aunty Eugie appeared at the door. She was still looking cross and drawn. She couldn't afford to go back on her decision but it was difficult to be so hard when there were few pleasures she could afford to give either of them.

'When that boy comes, tell him I want to speak to him.'

'If Grip goes, couldn't we keep Becky?' begged David.

'She's a wild animal. She's going to grow a lot bigger. You can't really keep her in a little backyard and expect her to be happy. This will be like a prison for her after a while. There's not even a blade of grass.'

'Please, Aunty,' began May, needing to try again, but she received such a look that she went no further. It was like asking for the moon.

As soon as Dudley arrived that afternoon, his face red from running, his dark eyes joyful, he knew that something was wrong. He said nothing when he was told he must either take Grip home or not expect to see him again. His whole expression changed, he looked utterly crushed.

'What are you going to do?' May asked him when Aunty Eugie had gone in again.

'I'll take him back.'

'And what'll happen?'

He shrugged. He knew but he couldn't tell May. He could hardly speak for the pain in his chest and he wished he could be alone with Grip, alone for ever. David was telling him about Becky's banishment, too, but he hardly heard him, his head empty of everything but his dread for Grip.

'Couldn't you show us where Becky came from?' David asked him. 'Her home must have been somewhere at The Crags. Perhaps if we took her back there she'd be able to manage. We could go back with you this afternoon. You could show us.'

Both May and David sensed the change in Dudley. He had clamped up, become again the boy they had first known, uncommunicative, brooding. It was as if all the days of friendship and laughter hadn't existed or had been forgotten. His eyes were dead and dark again, his face hard, as he sat beside Grip and stroked him fiercely.

May went and sat beside him. 'Come on,' she encouraged gently. 'Anything's better than the police station. There's no hope for him at all there.'

Dudley got up. 'Come on, lad,' he said to Grip, untying his rope. The dog's eyes were bright with eagerness.

'Won't you show us where Becky came from?' May asked him. 'Can't we come with you?'

'If tha likes,' he replied with gruff reluctance. 'It's near the pond. I'll show thee.'

Becky was so used to being in David's arms that it wasn't necessary to put her in a sack. He held her against his chest, under his pullover, and although she wriggled for a while, somewhat squashed, she soon grew quiet, more asleep than awake after having spent the night demolishing her den and trying to demolish Grip, too.

They had very little to say all the way to The Crags. May kept her eyes on Grip as if she were never going to see him again, David was thinking only of Becky, and Dudley felt as though his heart would burst, so savagely did it contract within him.

They went through the woods and after searching near the pond for a while, assisted by Grip who was very excited at being back near his old home again, they came across the ruins of the set that had been Becky's home. David had been afraid to put Becky on the ground, sure she would run off and lose herself in the bracken, but she was restless again, aware of the smells and sounds of her homeland and David's arms ached from carrying her.

When he at last put her down she was bewildered and nervous, clinging to Grip's heels as if afraid to lose him. But after a while her confidence grew and she began to explore. Whether she remembered her old home or not it was impossible to tell. To the watching children it looked as though she was making constant discoveries, whickering in her throat all the time.

Grip trotted back and forth among the trees and undergrowth, sometimes following the badger, sometimes being followed. Dudley didn't call him to heel. He stood somewhat apart from the others, hands in pockets, longing for them to go, wanting to face his father and Madman alone. He was too much aware of the closeness of them to care whether the badger found its old home and took to it, or not. Becky's fortunes or misfortunes were nothing to him.

David found an undemolished entrance to the old set and began to examine it excitedly, Grip beside him snuffling his nose down the tunnel, waving his tail, but Becky had found an old badger trail and was off on an exploration of her own. All of a sudden she came hurtling

back along the path, screeching with terror, instinctively
heading straight for the entrance David had found, almost
knocking both boy and dog off their feet. The fear she
emitted hung thickly on the air.

Grip stared towards the undergrowth, good ear pricked,
body quivering, intensely alert. There was a challenge in
his foursquare stance that Dudley quickly recognized. He
had seen it so many times before, in his father's dog, and

even as he understood what had happened, heart clenching within him, Madman appeared between the trees, pushing aside ferns and grasses with his tough, resolute shoulders, padding along at a steady pace in pursuit of the badger, not fast but determined.

He halted when he came to the clearing where the children and Grip were standing, instinctively defending the crumbled set where Becky had taken refuge, and even as he paused May and David could tell that this was no ordinary dog on an outing. Their skin prickled at the very aura of menace he exuded. They were frightened.

Madman's eyes fixed on Grip, the badger he had unexpectedly started up forgotten, and Grip, instead of running, wrinkled his lips into a snarl, aware of the fear-crazed badger and the trembling children, knowing he must protect them.

When Grip took his first ten paces towards Madman, hackles up, body swelling almost invisibly until the flesh was so tight under the skin that there was nothing loose for teeth to cling to, Dudley's agitated heart couldn't help but register a thrill of anticipation. Grip was facing Madman. He wasn't running. Whatever the outcome no one could ever call him a coward again.

The last battle

May and David had seen the odd skirmish between dogs in the park or on the street – a collision, a crescendo of hysterical barks and growls, a flurry of bodies and then usually a break away with one of the dogs running off, often pursued by the other for a few yards with rarely a second engagement. Once Jenny started a fight with a dog that poked its muzzle inside their front door and Aunty Eugie had had to throw a bucket of water over them to separate them, but even as they watched the two bull terriers stalk up to each other, slowly, warily, calm even while they snarled, they knew that this confrontation had nothing in common with those street battles, as short as they were noisy.

The dogs circled each other, growls rising and dying in their throats as each looked for his enemy's weakness or strength. Madman started all his battles like this. Even though his confidence was supreme he never flung himself hot-headedly into any fight and, as always, from the very beginning dominated the whole proceedings, the very threat in his movements causing his opponent to take up a defensive attitude instead of preparing himself for attack.

At this point May cried out, 'Surely you can stop them!' not realizing that as far as the dogs were concerned battle had already commenced. But she understood from Dudley's expression at least that he wouldn't stop them, even if he could. He was with Grip heart and soul. Everybody and everything else was forgotten.

Suddenly Madman made a flashing lunge towards Grip's stifle which he escaped with an equally quick backward spring, followed by his own thrusting forward at his enemy's temporarily exposed throat. These first two movements were to be the basis of the whole struggle, Madman lunging constantly for Grip's back legs, the other responding with an attack at Madman's throat. Either spot was equally vulnerable and each animal knew it.

Sometimes they closed in furiously for several seconds, fighting shoulder to shoulder. At other times they separated widely then came back in a rush, using brusque shoulder movements in an attempt to throw the other off balance. There was an uncanny similarity in their movements, with Grip looking more and more like his sire as the heat of the combat fired his spirit. Ears flattened, eyes glazed, he fought and held and broke away, lips pulled back to show fangs as terrible as Madman's.

Dudley's face was red with emotion and his heart swelled with pride. Madman had some seven years of fighting behind him, with all the experience of triumph after triumph. Grip had only his breeding and his instinct. He was still fighting defensively, holding his own but no more, with Madman harrying him on every side, trying to wear him down. No blood was spilled. Neither dog went in for useless slashings. Each looked for the one sure grip that would be final. Now and again they growled but mostly they were silent, except for sharp grunts or heavy pantings in moments when they broke away of mutual accord.

They were like two prize-fighters, closing in, separating, looking for and avoiding the death-hold, careless of time. Madman looked the stronger of the two. He was six pounds heavier and twice in the first few minutes he knocked Grip off his feet with shoulder charges. Had he been a bit more agile he would have had Grip then, at his most defenceless, but Grip was six years younger and that much swifter.

Dudley didn't know at what point in the battle his father arrived. He looked up and saw him on the other side of the clearing, as intent and inflamed as he was, unable to believe his eyes. Grip and Madman fighting it out was something he no longer expected to see but, after his initial amazement, he forgot everything but the fever of the fight, jealously watching for Madman's superiority but having to admit to himself that the blood of the father was strong in the son.

Although Grip hadn't yet begun a single attack, he was holding his own with forceful courage. Round and round they went, back and forth, with hardly a pause for breath. Ten minutes drew into twenty and then became thirty and still neither had found the hold he wanted. Madman had ripped Grip's ear again and his blood was on both of them, streaking their bodies, and Grip had split Madman's lips in a head to head clash. But they were as strong as ever, with Grip learning fast now and anticipating Madman's movements before they came.

It was Grip's turn to instigate each new attack after a break away, charging in with a determination where blind fury played no part. Neither of the dogs fought with anger, only with unquenchable stubbornness, and more than once Madman found himself on the defensive, giving ground instead of making it.

At this point the fight grew more intense. Grip had abandoned all defensive action and Madman would give way no more. They fought it out face to face, sometimes standing high on their back legs then suddenly dropping down with their heads on the ground, each trying to take

advantage of the other, neither succeeding. The lips of
both were slashed and bleeding. Their eyes were glazed.

They broke away for a few moments. Had this been an
organized contest their seconds would have rushed in at
this point to cart them off and refresh them with a sponging down, but this was a thing between Grip and Madman
alone. Both were weary. Grip had never been in a sus-
tained battle before and he could hardly move while he

panted in a state bordering on exhaustion. Madman had great endurance but for a long time he hadn't been pressed so hard. He too panted and rested, the saliva that dripped from his jaws stained pink like Grip's.

May and David were no longer watching. Bill Kershaw had gone up to them at some time during the fight, suddenly aware of the girl's distress and her brother's pale, shocked face and, with an expression as fierce as his words, told them to get out of it and not come back. They had run off immediately, May crying, David not daring to argue, and Dudley hadn't even noticed.

While the dogs rested he glanced at his father again and met his challenging expression with equal defiance.

'If he wins,' said Bill Kershaw, 'tha can do what tha likes with him. That's a promise. But he won't win. Madman's got too much pride to let that sprat get the better of him.'

'He'll win,' was all Dudley could answer.

Then their eyes were drawn to the dogs again, once more shoulder to shoulder, each trying to get his own hold on while keeping off the other's, and it looked as though Grip had discovered a new trick for enticing his opponent towards him. Cheek on the ground, rump in the air, he waited for Madman to come into the attack, ready to spring at his throat which would be above him from such a position. It was a stance both self-protecting and attacking but it left his hindquarters undefended unless he could move them round swiftly while keeping his head on the ground. This he managed to do a couple of times but not without losing the advantage of the lower head position. The third time Madman rushed in at him, making straight for his stifle, he flung himself upward and at last found the hold he had been seeking all along.

His teeth closed on Madman's throat but, at the same time, the impetus of the other dog's rush carried him on to the hold he had been seeking and which Grip in that moment had neglected to defend. Madman's teeth took hold of Grip's thigh, too high up for him to crack the bone instantly, but with Grip's weight on his throat, holding him back, he was unable to change his position. Grip's hold, too, was not of the best, being too low down either to choke him or to tear open the jugular, but each dog had a hold and neither intended to release it.

Then came the hardest part for Dudley and his father. Both knew that only one of the two animals would come out of the grip they had set on each other. Either Madman would manage to inch his jaws down a little or Grip would inch his up. Grip would slowly throttle Madman if Madman couldn't first lame him and then throw him off. Madman still had four legs to stand on, Grip only three and with one of his front legs of little use because of the way he was twisted. They moved very slowly, if at all, not wanting to relinquish one hold until sure of the next, Madman with forty-five pounds of dog dragging at his throat, hampering his jaws, keeping him from his crunching victory, so near and yet so far.

To Dudley their heavy panting seemed like heartbeats pulsing away. His own heart raced in a way that made his head spin and his legs feel as though they didn't belong to him. He couldn't even cry out Grip's name or a word of encouragement, not that anything he said or did now would make any difference. He didn't look at his father, didn't even remember him, and he had to rub his eyes because of the blinding sweat that ran into them from his forehead.

Grip made a movement, tottering as he did so, but his jaws were that much closer than before. Madman could do nothing and if there was any inkling in any part of him, instinct perhaps, that this might be his last battle he gave no sign of it. He stood foursquare, except when Grip, tottering still, pulled him down, but although his head went down his legs maintained their position.

Bit by bit Grip's jaws crept up and soon the hold that Madman had on his thigh was loosened; slowly, very slowly, as slowly as the gradual closing of his windpipe because Bill Kershaw's dog, as proud as he was wicked, would never admit that he was beaten. Madman's teeth relinquished their hold altogether but even when Grip's thigh had slipped from his grasp he still stood there, solid, unmoving, making no effort to tug away, as if unable to believe that the last hold wasn't his. His understanding was already leaving him, cut off from oxygen. Death would come before any realization of defeat.

'I'll call him off,' cried Dudley suddenly, at this last minute not bearing to see Madman's death.

'Nay,' shouted his father, his voice far harsher than usual and with a note in which Dudley recognized his own anguish. 'Let things be. He'd rather go this way than any other.'

Dudley knew this was true and so he stood and watched, the tears running down his cheeks for Madman although he had hated him until now.

Nothing to fight

It wasn't until the last day of the holidays that May and David saw Dudley again. They had been back to the woods at The Crags several times to look for Becky but to no avail. She wasn't at the old set and there were no signs of her anywhere else. They could only hope she had found a new home for herself somewhere where she would be happier than in the backyard at Mill Cottages.

'Well, at least I had her for a while,' David said, more to console himself than May. 'I always did want a badger.'

Neither of them had gone to look for Dudley. May had been so upset by the fight that for nights she had dreamed violently of the two dogs, waking with tears and trembling hands. They had said nothing to Aunty Eugie, mostly out of loyalty to Dudley. They knew he loved his dog, even if it was in a way they couldn't understand, and they had sensed that afternoon in the woods that the fight between the two dogs was something that had had to come, a reckoning long awaited.

It had frightened both of them and made them understand why Dudley was different from them in so many ways. He had lived always with violence, they with gentleness. They were afraid to step into his world again and they both tried to put him out of their minds.

It wasn't easy for May not to think of Grip. She loved him and wondered far too often what the result of that fight at The Crags had been. So she dreamed and cried and woke in the night to light the candle at her bedside with shivering fingers, and if Aunty Eugie guessed it had something to do with the dog she said nothing, not knowing how to console her, believing that time would bring its comfort as it always did.

It wasn't time but Dudley himself who finally brought the smiles back to May. He appeared at the back door on the very last day of the holidays, Grip beside him, looking as strong and handsome as he ever had, as if that death battle in the woods had never taken place.

Both were welcomed in with cries of delight, as well as the usual bread and dripping, and even David consented to stay and listen to their talk, May's mostly because, as usual, she answered most of the questions herself. Dudley briefly told them that Madman was dead and comforted May by assuring her that Grip would fight no more.

'I'm going to put him at stud, like tha said, remember?' he told her. 'He's got a first-class reputation now, as well as breeding. But I'll not fight him. I won't have him end up like Madman.'

When he said this he was thinking of his father who, in his way and in spite of his hardness, had loved Madman as much as he himself loved Grip, as ever he had managed to love anything. You couldn't help loving something that was with you constantly, that was all your pride. Dudley had suffered enough for Grip already and didn't want any more.

'Will your father get another dog?' May asked, curious as always.

Dudley shook his head. 'I don't know, but there'll never be another dog like Madman. Not even Grip's like him really. He hasn't got the fighting spirit Madman had. He's better in a lot of ways but . . .' He stopped, trying to find the right words to explain himself. 'Bull terriers were meant for fighting but, bit by bit, there's nowt left for them to fight.'

'Oh, I'm glad you're not going to fight any more,' cried May, pulling Grip towards her and rubbing her head against him. 'Do you remember me?' she demanded, looking into his black eyes.

And Grip stretched out his big tongue to lick her face, making her laugh in delight. Dudley laughed too, especially when Grip jumped on top of him and pinned him down with half a dozen slobbering licks, cleaning off the dripping on his chin.